STRANDED!

Presented to

JAMIE MACKAY
by
URQUHART &

GLENMORISTON

SUNDAY CLUB
4th JUNE 2000

STRANDED!

CATHIE BARTLAM

Scripture Union
130 City Road, London EC1V 2NJ.

By the same author:
Operation Sandy – Tiger Book
Tricky Business – Tiger Book
Go for Gold – Leopard Book

© Cathie Bartlam 1991
First published 1991

ISBN   0 86201 681 9

Phototypeset by Input Typesetting Ltd, London
Printed and bound in Great Britain by Cox and Wyman Ltd, Reading

Chapter One

'Right, Ian. It's your turn.'

Ian couldn't wait. At last the moment had arrived that he had dreamed about for months. In a few minutes he would be flying; skimming across the dark blue lake like a bird.

'Move up to the front. Careful!' Uncle Steve grabbed his arm as Ian nearly catapulted through the walk-through windshield that led to the bows of the speed boat. 'Okay, squat down while I fix the skis on.'

Ian thrust his bare pale feet into the stiff rubber bindings while his uncle adjusted them.

'You know what to do?'

Ian nodded. Course he did. Months studying *Waterskiing for beginners* was about to prove useful.

'Over the side then.'

Ian hesitated. 'How?'

'You dollop!' called Aunt Lynda, sitting in front of the steering wheel. 'You've got one ski on top of the other.'

Ian lifted his left leg and immediately fell over. Picking himself up, with great difficulty, he glowered at his sister Julia and his two cousins who were laughing at him from the back of the boat.

'Get a move on,' yelled Dave. 'It's my turn next. We'll be here all day.'

Lunging himself over the bow of the bobbing blue

and white boat, Ian felt the cold water seep into his wet-suit, sending icy shivers travelling through his body. At last he was in the water, the buoyancy jacket keeping him the right way up as he fought the huge, heavy planks of wood strapped to his feet.

'Now, take your time.' Uncle Steve's face loomed over him. 'Don't shout "Go" till you're sure you are ready. I'll be watching. Just do it like I did.'

'Okay,' Ian called back, managing to get his breathing back to normal. He didn't feel so cold now. As Aunt Lynda started the engine, the boat moved away from him in a big circle.

'Here it comes!' Uncle Steve expertly threw the striped tow-rope across the water. Funny, the lake was going up and down a lot more, now that Ian was actually in it.

Slowly, so slowly the tow-rope crept nearer. Ian grabbed it, letting it run through his fingers, until the black plastic handle was firmly grasped in his thick strong fingers.

Ian's excitement began to be mixed with fear. Just do it, like Uncle Steve. Body in correct position, skis at right angle with the tips just showing, knees bent, arms straight. In his mind he could see the drawing in the book, but his wet-suited body didn't want to do what his brain told it.

'Keep still,' Ian hissed at the bouncing skis, that seemed to have a mind of their own. His teeth were chattering with a combination of cold, excitement, suspense and fear. A thick slick of pale blond hair was plastered over his left eye. He dare not push it out of the way, in case he lost the handle.

Eventually Ian decided he was ready. Boat straight ahead, tow-rope in a slack line between his skis. Legs, knees, arms braced.

'Ready?' yelled Uncle Steve.

This was it. Ian Rathbone was about to ski the length of Lake Windermere!

Just as he shouted 'Go! Hit it!' the thought flashed through his mind. How would he know when to stop?

He need not have worried. In the space of one and a half seconds he flew upright into the air and straight back down onto the hard lake surface. Flat on his face he felt one ski tear off and the other drag his foot down. After thrashing about, he turned himself the right way up, rescued the ski – at £200 a pair, he'd better not lose them – and assured the returning boat that he was fine.

'Wonderful,' called Dave, grinning. 'So stylish, so graceful.'

'Ah, shut up!' Ian gulped a mouthful of lake in shouting at his cousin.

'Another go?' queried Uncle Steve.

'Right on.'

The next go was no better. Ian couldn't understand it. *Water-skiing for beginners* had promised that it would work. As the boat circled for his third attempt, Ian went through the process in his mind again. It was obvious. He wasn't holding the handle tight enough.

After five minutes, while Dave got impatient, Ian decided that he was ready for his next attempt. He stared hard at the back end of the boat, the throbbing 125 horse power engine waiting to be released into its full potential. This time he'd do it. He'd slice across the water, his skis' wake mingling with that of the boats.

Ian was right. For a full eleven seconds he was towed across the lake. The only trouble was that he was flat on his stomach, his freckled chin sending a tiny wake to bubble harmlessly by his stretched and aching body.

He could hear people shouting and screeching. At last the words 'Let go' penetrated his fumbled brain. Ian saw his pale knuckles gleaming in the sunlight, as he watched his hands release the tow-rope handle. It was as if his arms weren't part of him.

His frantic rush through the blackening water came to a halt and Ian lay there, shattered, angry, humiliated. His arms felt as if they'd been pulled out of their sockets and his front felt as if a steam roller had flattened him. It was a good job Uncle Steve had insisted he wear the buoyancy jacket. Otherwise Ian would have let himself plunge beneath the surface and quietly drown. He felt such an idiot. And where on earth, or to be more accurate, where on lake, were the skis?

'You okay?' Aunt Lynda's piercing voice reached him.

He nodded, which was useless as no-one could tell what he was doing.

'I got two or three of it,' Julia, his older sister called, waving her camera. 'They'll be brilliant, if they come out.'

'Should have seen yourself,' Dave laughed. 'Wait till we tell the others on the caravan site. "Ian Rathbone, tum-skiing specialist!"'

Uncle Steve looked a bit cross. 'First rule,' he shouted, 'always let go. We'll get the skis, if we can find them, and come back for you. Wait there!'

Wait there! The morons. Where did they think he was going? Perhaps he felt like a ten mile swim the length of Windermere while they retrieved their precious skis? Or he might potter off fishing!

Ian quietly trod water, wondering what he was doing, in the middle of a lake, miles from home, on holiday with his manic cousins. On the lakeshore he could see the smudgy browns and greens of the woodlands, and in the distance some looming mountains. Nearer the shore someone else was skiing, figures of eight, perfect. Why not me? he thought. I wanted to do it, to show them I could. I wanted to be really good and all I've done is make a right fool of myself. It's not fair! For weeks, no months, I've practised, doing sit-ups, getting my muscles strong and now *I can't do it!*

The boat returned.

'Another go?' asked Ian hopefully.

'I think you've had your share. It's David's turn,' said Uncle Steve, letting the swim platform down at the back of the boat for Ian to clamber on to. 'Better luck next time.'

Ian stood dripping on the platform as Dave stripped him of his jacket and urged him to get the wet-suit off. One problem was that they had got to share the suit. It was really hard to peel the wet sticky rubber off with goose pimpled hands. And even harder to watch Dave slip into it, ready for his attempt to ski Windermere.

Of course, Dave could do it. But then he would. He'd been coming here to Windermere for years, and he was older than Ian. Only a few months, but being nearly thirteen, Dave thought he knew everything. Ian watched his sleek, dark-haired cousin twist through the water and a stab of envy struck him, as Dave turned to wave. Ian had to admit that he looked good, just like he, Ian, should have done. Instead, what had he looked like? A dying duck in a thunderstorm!

'He's really come on, this year,' said Uncle Steve, carefully observing him. 'You know, Ian, it was two summers before David managed to get upright. Mind you, he was younger then.'

'I'll do it next time.'

'Course you will. Just promise me you'll let go, eh?'

Ian smiled and rubbed his reddened chest, now hidden by an outsize T-shirt.

'Yes, Uncle Steve,' he answered, like a three year old. 'I'm starving!'

'Under the seat,' called Aunt Lynda.

'What?'

'Food. Julia, Bev, shift out of the way.'

Ian leaned forward and pushed Julia off her seat, the

boat moved suddenly and he found himself on Bev's lap. He shot off like a rocket, but it was too late. He was smeared with thick, smelly sun-tan oil. Bev was a right poser and seemed to view the back of the boat as a mobile sun-bathing platform. If the girls had wanted to laze around, they should have stayed at the caravan site, not cluttered up the boat.

'You fat plonker! Stay still,' Julia screeched.

'Shut up, Julia. It's Bev's fault,' said Ian.

Bev just smiled. 'Okay, no hassle.' She stretched under the padded seat and produced cans of pop and a packet of biscuits.

Ian sat watching Dave. He'd only fallen over a couple of times and waited patiently while the boat circled back round to him. Absent-mindedly passing the half-way stage on the biscuits, Ian started day-dreaming. That wasn't Dave out there. Oh, no. It was him, feeling the rush of the air past his ears, the taut pull of the rope on his arms, the controlling power of cruising over the water and the gentle spray tickling his face. It was him that everyone was watching.

'Oh, isn't he brave.'

'Just look at that!'

'Straight over the wake, too.'

'And not yet thirteen!'

Look at the way Uncle Steve was watching Dave. So proud. So smiley. Ian couldn't remember when his own dad had ever looked at him like that. In fact he couldn't remember Dad, or Mum for that matter, smiling for ages. That was why he and Julia were on holiday with their cousins. Give Mum and Dad a break. See if it was worth trying again. Trying what? Odd snatches of conversation forced their way into his reluctant mind . . . no point going on . . . you should have married your job . . . doors slamming . . . tears.

Ian stuffed his hands over his ears. He wouldn't think

about Them. It hurt too much. Back to being water ski champion of Windermere. The new find. The amazing Ian Rathbone skis Windermere, the Channel, the Atlantic! Mind you, you'd starve to death, skiing the Atlantic. Ten metres on the lake would do, to start with.

The boat had stopped and Dave was struggling to climb aboard. His thick, dark curls were plastered to his deep-tanned face and he looked well pleased with himself.

'Did you see that. Straight over the wake without a fall. Brill!'

'Sit down,' his mum called, not turning her head. How did mums get this ability to see what was going on without looking, thought Ian.

'Make sure that rope's in.' Everything was carefully stowed away. 'We'll head back. Get your heads down and keep still. Let's go!' She turned and grinned as she opened up the throttle.

The boat, a Cobra, leapt into the air and galloped diagonally across the water. Great foaming, creamy waves of wake veered off behind them, sending air bubbles into the greeny depths below. The boat bucked and reared over the wakes of other boats. Ian forgot his disappointment as he clung to the padded grey seat, enjoying the surge of power vibrating through the fibreglass hull and every part of him. It was fantastic! Could you imagine skiing at that speed?

The boat slowed to a dawdle as they approached the six mile per hour limit near the islands. As they threaded their way through the hired brown wooden rowing boats and little launches with 'put-put' engines, Ian felt great. He felt dead superior to the other lake users. This was his boat, his territory.

'Watch your side.' Uncle Steve's voice brought him back to reality as they docked at the caravan site's jetty. 'Lynda, why don't you and the girls make some tea?

11

David and Ian can help me.'

'Helping' was fun, but harder work than Ian had bargained for. The skis and jackets had to be stored, the boat given a clean over and then the stiff, unyielding grey canvas cover had to be battened and pulled into place. Finally Uncle Steve was satisfied.

'Right, you two, the shower block, and take this with you.' He passed them the wet-suit. 'Give it a rinse and bring it back to the caravan, or else.'

'Okay,' chorused the boys.

The shower was heaven. Ian realised how tired he was. It was sevenish. He'd been up fifteen hours, had that monotonous motorway journey, arrived here for a late breakfast and been out on the boat all day. His whole body ached and tingled as the delicious hot water rained down on him.

'You're good, Dave,' he called to the next cubicle. 'Really good.'

'Ta, mate, You'll be okay, too.'

'You think so?'

'Sure. A few more tries, you'll be flying.'

'You're right. Hurry up. I'm starved.'

They'd forgotten their dry clothes, so raced back to the caravan wrapped in towels. Soon they sat down to the biggest heap of sausage and mash they'd ever seen. As Ian wolfed down his fifth sausage, liberally smothered in tomato sauce, he turned to his uncle.

'Can we go out again tomorrow?'

'Of course. Bev and Julia's turn first, though.'

'Oh, right.'

'Hurry up. Let's get an early night. It's been a long day.'

Ian shuffled into his bunk bed, staring at the snoring lump above him that was Dave. Just a few more goes. I'll be flying, he thought, as he drifted off to sleep.

Chapter Two

Ian woke early the next morning and lay quietly in his bunk trying to remember where he was. Sunlight was already edging its way through the gap in the curtains. A bird in army boots was patrolling the caravan roof. Ian sat up, banged his head on the top bunk and slid out of his sleeping bag. Of course. Here, Windermere. Seven whole days of speed-boats, swimming, snorkelling and skiing.

No-one else was awake. How could they possibly stay asleep when miles of open lake lay waiting for them? Ian crept out of the caravan, clad in his pyjama trousers. Spying the wet-suits on the rack, he helped himself to Dave's and wriggled into it. That way he would be bound to have first go in the water.

I'll go down to the boat, he thought. Make sure it's all right.

He forced his feet into his old wet trainers, that were lying underneath the caravan, and walked proudly to the jetty. He really felt the part. The navy and grey sleeveless wet-suit was damp and clammy but clung to him tightly. It smoothed out the lumpy bumpy bits round his waist and made his blue eyes seem to sparkle in the early morning light. He tried to bring his thick blond hair under control, by spitting on his hands and rubbing them over his head. It did little for his image.

The smell of bacon wafted from some caravans, radios

were playing, one or two people smiled and said 'Good morning' as they walked to the site shop. Ian said 'Hello' to everyone. They'd all know him soon, the clever kid on the water skis.

Ian sat on the jetty looking around him. As yet no boats ruffled the calm surface of the lake. A wispy mist was slowly climbing up the hills.

It was going to be a glorious day. In between the bouncing moored boats mallards and a pair of swans foraged, ducking down through the greasy water to salvage bits of abandoned sandwiches, in preference to hunting for food further out. Sparrows constantly flitted around, restless, landing right by Ian and taking off in the same breath. Watching them Ian felt strangely at peace. You'd never catch him sitting like this at home. Too much football to play there.

He was just in the middle of his favourite day-dream, one-handed skiing, cheered on by all his mates, when Julia's voice shattered the silence.

'Thought I might find you here. Breakfast in a few minutes.'

Ian looked up at blue eyes just like his and long blond hair, today swinging in a high pony tail. He would never understand girls. Why waste a morning like this putting all that make-up on?

'Come on. They might get cross if we're late.'

'Late?' queried Ian.

'You'll never believe it,' said Julia, matching her stride to his and looking straight at him. 'After breakfast, we're going to church.'

'Church?'

'Church.'

'On holiday? Come off it.'

'Look, don't fuss. You know what they're like. All the God stuff.'

'But on holiday? They can forget it!'

14

'Perhaps we'd better just go along. I mean, I think it's crazy, but if we upset them now, there might be an awful row. And they're dead nice, really.'

Ian was thoughtful. Awful rows were the last thing he wanted – but church on a day like today was a very hard price to pay for not having a row. To tell the truth the only worry he'd had about coming on holiday was in case they came heavy on the God stuff. I mean, they're all as bad, he thought. Even Dave. He says prayers. I ask you, nearly thirteen and talks to someone who isn't even there. At least he's never tried to get me to pray . . . and he'd better not start now.

'Ah, Ian, breakfast.' Aunt Lynda eyed him curiously. 'I don't think you'll be needing that outfit just yet.'

'Why?' he questioned.

'Bit uncomfortable for church.'

'I'll just hang around by the jetty . . . ouch.' Ian rubbed his ankle where Julia had kicked him.

'We'd like you both to come with us,' said Uncle Steve softly. Ian turned and was relieved to see his uncle wearing a sports shirt and shorts. At least he hadn't got to dress up for church. 'We'll take the boat out after dinner, don't worry.'

Don't worry! After dinner! That was hours away. How could anyone choose to spend a hot summer's morning at church and cooking dinner? Dad was right when he said his sister, Aunt Lynda, was a religious nut. However, eleven o'clock found Ian in church for the first time in his life, if you didn't count two weddings, one christening and a school trip to Coventry Cathedral. He had never felt so bored. While the people, and he had to admit there were a lot of them, stood up, sat down, and sang songs he'd never heard of, Ian amused himself. He tried to work out how old the vicar was and counted the pieces in a stained glass window at the front.

The seats were hard. I bet it's to stop you falling

asleep, he thought, wriggling around and finally sitting on his hands.

Someone prayed and thanked God for the beautiful hot summer they were enjoying. Ian was cross. Why talk about it, why not get out there and *use* it? Anyway, anyone with an ounce of common sense knew it was hot because a band of high pressure was stretched across Britain. What it had to do with God was beyond him.

The vicar, who looked like Batman with his cloak, was waffling on. Ian's mind was concentrating on his water-skiing technique, or rather lack of it, but a few words seemed to bounce into his mind. They didn't make sense, but they stuck there. 'The Son of Man came to seek and to save the lost.' Batman was telling stories about lost things that got found, a sheep, a runaway son, a gold coin. This seemed to interest the people around him, but not Ian. He was just curious about the Son of Man, whoever he was.

'Dave,' he nudged his cousin. 'Who's the Son of Man?'

'Jesus, you know. It's another name for him.'

Strange, thought Ian. Why bother having two names?

At last the service was over. Uncle Steve and Batman chatted away like old friends.

'And who is this?' asked Batman, beaming at him.

'My nephew, Ian.'

'Ah, good to have you with us. Did you like the service?'

Ian tried to be diplomatic. 'Er . . . well . . . yea . . . sort of. The Son of Man was good.' That should impress him, and shut him up.

'Yes, wonderful to know that Jesus came to save us all.'

'Wonderful,' echoed Ian. He hadn't a clue what Batman was on about. He didn't need saving, by anyone. Ian wanted to get out of the place, so he swung round and joined Bev outside.

Dinner took ages to get ready. Then they sat there talking, mostly about the service. All except Ian. Even Julia joined in.

'What you up to,' Ian got hold of her later, on the way to the boat, 'joining in all that God talk?'

'You could learn, little brother,' Julia patted him on his head although he was as tall as her. 'Talk their language and they'll leave you alone. It's like playing a game. Amen! Hallelujah!' and she tickled him in the ribs.

'Right on,' Ian caught the idea. Just agree with anything they said, and carry on as normal.

At last the boat was chugging its way out into the lake.

'Bit of sightseeing first,' Aunt Lynda informed them.

Ian groaned.

'We'll go the other way, past Belle Island. Look! You can just see the round tower . . . and over there is Bowness pier.'

How absolutely fascinating! thought Ian.

'We'll turn at the ferry.' At least the slow moving ferry clanking along on its heavy greased cables held Ian's attention for a moment.

'Do you know,' chipped in Uncle Steve, 'that in 1635 the ferry sank and forty seven people drowned.'

'And,' said Dave, 'on wild stormy nights the ghostly "Crier of Claife" can be heard calling the boat. Then he haunts the ferryman to his death.'

'Gerroff it,' said Ian.

'It's true, isn't it, Dad?'

'So they say. Ever since a ferry nan returned one night terrified, struck dumb and then died a few days later. So make sure,' Uncle Steve tried to leer threateningly, but only managed to look daft, 'that you never wander the Claife shore on a dark windy night.'

I don't want to wander any shore, thought Ian, just belt along the lake. If I'd wanted a cruise, I could have done a trip on one of the pleasure steamers. For goodness sake, get a move on, he silently screamed, let's have a go at water-skiing.

After what seemed an absolute age they reached the water-skiing area. Ian got up.

'Not so fast,' said Uncle Steve. 'Girls first. Julia? Bev?'

'Not me today,' said Bev. She was lying stretched out in suntop and shorts, toasting herself even darker brown. Her brown curls were hidden under a scarf to stop 'the ends drying out'. 'My mascara will run. Perhaps later.'

'I'll have a go, Uncle Steve,' Julia stood up. Ian did some rapid calculations. At least an hour before Julia would have finished making a fool of herself. Why couldn't she sunbathe as well?

'Here, just wear the wet-suit jacket, and the buoyancy jacket. It's quite warm today.' Uncle Steve kitted her out. 'Now in you get. Watch the side of the boat with the skis.'

Julia Rathbone, netball captain, tennis player, trampolinist and half way through taking ten, yes ten, GCSE's rolled gracefully into the water.

'Know what to do?'

'Not really.'

For someone who firstly didn't know what to do, and secondly wasn't that bothered, Julia had all the luck. On her third attempt she was up, admittedly for only a few seconds. But up. Ian was furious. Life wasn't fair. His stupid sister was better than him. They were all better than him. Fortunately no-one noticed him sulking. They were all too busy telling Julia how marvellous she was.

Then it was Uncle Steve's turn. Brilliant, of course. Then David. Ian couldn't believe it. Even Aunt Lynda was having a go. Ian had never seen anyone take so long to remove one skirt and replace it with one wet-suit jacket and a pair of shorts.

'Now, not too fast, Steve. David, you watch the rope. You'll be the observer. Don't go until I'm ready.'

At last she was ready. Ian watched in amazement. Aunt Lynda, who must be forty years old, who was cuddly by anyone's standards and who had fat varicose veins up one of her legs, like blue biro marks, could water-ski. A bit wobbly, but she could do it. And he, Ian, didn't look like getting a chance. Water-skiing was for young people, not aged crones, he thought nastily.

By the time his turn came Ian was like a steam engine, full of pent up frustration and anger. He'd do it, if it killed him. If anything he was worse than the previous day. He just couldn't get it together. His legs did what they pleased, the buoyancy jacket was too loose and the shoulders were higher than his ears. He missed the tow-rope and when he did get into position, he fell over every time the boat zoomed off.

After eight attempts, Uncle Steve made him give up.

'You're too tired now. I think we've had enough.'

Ian started to answer back.

'No arguing. I'll tell you what, why don't we have a swim? Stay right by the boat. Come on you lazy lot, Bev, Julia, shift, so I can stow the skis away.'

So the four cousins spent the next hour diving off the swim platform, and shrieking around the stationary boat, while Aunt Lynda fell asleep and Uncle Steve took his role as coastguard very seriously.

'Race you to the bottom,' called Ian to Dave.

'You daft bat. Know how deep it is?'

'What then, clever clogs?'

'About seventy metres, that's what.'

'Seventy metres!' Ian had second thoughts about reaching the bottom.

Just think, below him was water, just water. He lay on his back. And above him was blue, blue sky, for

19

miles. Maybe Uncle Steve's God was up there some-where. Ian felt very small in the moving vastness of the lake.

'Anyway, the pike'll get you.'

'Or the eels,' added Bev.

'Enormous. Metres long. Thick as tree trunks.'

'And pike with teeth like crocodiles!'

'Oh, yea,' said Ian. They must think he was daft.

Ian was happy again. He was a good swimmer, as were the others, and eventually it was time to climb aboard and roar back to the jetty.

'Late supper,' shouted Uncle Steve, as they went towards the shower block. 'Go and enjoy yourselves.'

So after a quick shower, Dave and Ian set off to explore the woods by the site. Dave knew every inch of the grounds, he came here so often. Ian pretended he wasn't that interested but really his eyes were taking in all that he could see. Some ace trees for climbing and bushes to crawl into.

Suddenly Dave stopped.

'Ian, look up there.'

He looked but could not see anything, as the redden-ing sky sent dark shadows scuttling across the trees.

'What?'

'It's a bird.'

'Where?'

'Look, follow me. Now can you see it?'

Ian could see all right. He'd never seen one so close, in real life. The golden brown feathers on its chest vibrated with the effort of its beating wings. Its piercing brown eyes stared down at them over its curved lemon beak. And the wings frantically thrust through the still evening air. But this kestrel was going nowhere. The proud bird of prey hung upside down, helpless, held by the strong leather strap fastened to its leg. Caught up in the trees, getting weaker with every minute.

'What shall we do?' asked Ian.

'Save it. Set it free.'

'How? It's too high up.'

'I'll fetch Dad. You keep guard,' and Dave raced off through the wood, leaving Ian alone to watch the desperate bird as it grew rapidly darker.

Save it? But how?

Chapter Three

Ian walked up and down, keeping a constant watchful eye on the desperate bird. Why didn't Dave hurry up? After what seemed like hours he heard his cousin's voice calling through the darkening undergrowth, and with much crashing and stomping, Dave emerged from the bushes.

'They'll be here in a minute.'

'They?'

'Dad and Tom Fraser.'

'Tom Fraser?'

'Yes, he's a falconer, knows what to do.'

Uncle Steve appeared, clutching one end of a silvery aluminium ladder that gleamed oddly in the failing light. Tom Fraser supported the other end, and as the two men wriggled the ladder close to the kestrel, Ian watched.

'It's Batman!' he exclaimed.

'What did you say?' asked Dave.

'Nothing.' But it *was* Batman, Ian was sure. His eyes travelled up the figure now testing his weight against the ladder. Old trainers that might have been white a long time ago, with a hole in them, faded jeans, black T-shirt, a tanned face dominated by a huge pair of specs that looked as if they would fall off his thin nose any second, and all topped by a wad of straight brown hair that needed cutting. Batmen, no – vicars, were not supposed to look like this!

'You okay, Tom?' Uncle Steve was holding the ladder.

'I think so. If I go right to the top I might just reach her.' Tom Fraser's voice changed to a soft shushing sound as he talked to the bird, 'Hush, hush my beauty. Soon be free.'

Tom delved into the pocket of his jeans and produced a huge leather gauntlet and a red Stanley knife with a sharp blade.

'I'll have to cut the leather cord, the jess. You boys help to hold the ladder steady.'

Ian grabbed the edge of the ladder and bent his neck right back so he could see what was happening. It was amazing. Batman put his gloved hand out to the bird and in a split second the kestrel clawed its sharp talons into the leather and swung itself upright. The wings that had been going berserk stopped flapping, just like that. The kestrel was still, not moving.

'Is it dead?' called Ian.

'No, course not,' replied Tom, precariously balancing as he sawed away at the cord that still tied the bird to the tree. 'She knows that she is safe now.' He walked slowly backwards down the ladder and turned to face the boys.

'Look, she's fine now.'

Ian gazed at the beautiful brown bird inches from him. She stared at him with panic-free eyes, quietly sitting on Tom's hand. Only a heaving chest showed the exertion she had been through.

'No, don't!' Tom prevented Ian from touching her. 'Kestrel beaks and claws are really tough. That is why I've got this enormous glove on.'

'Why did she stop panicking when you got near her?' asked Dave, on the way back through the wood.

'She just knew she was safe. You see she's a trained kestrel. When she saw the gauntlet she knew she could perch on it. She knew it was something safe to hold on to.'

'Is she yours?'

'Oh, no. Can't keep these in a vicarage in town. No, she'll be from up the fells.'

'Fells?'

'The hills. She must have escaped. Look, see this ring here on her leg? Well, it has a number on and I can trace her owner from that.'

Uncle Steve was as interested as the boys.

'How do you know all about them – kestrels, I mean?' asked Ian.

'Bit of a hobby of mine. Sometimes I go up the fells where I know some of the farmers and I fly their birds. This is probably one of theirs.'

Ian realised that they were now walking through the town and as they turned into a pathway, he found himself at the vicarage. Church and a vicarage in one day! What would his mates think?

'I'll make us a drink,' said Batman. 'You boys can call me Tom.'

They followed him into the kitchen where every available surface was covered with mugs, bits of paper and piles of books. Tom unearthed a kettle and filled it, while the rest sat down at the scrubbed wooden table, also covered in books plus an ancient typewriter.

'It's my study,' said Tom, seeing their puzzled faces. 'Much friendlier to work in here than stuck in another room.' He had casually put the kestrel on the work surface where she immediately made a mess on a book entitled 'Eighteenth century sermons on the life of Saint Paul.'

'The bird!' exclaimed Ian.

'I'll put her in a box,' said Tom and he dived out of the room.

'He's fun,' commented Dave. 'Not like most people imagine a vicar. Look at the junk in here!'

'Makes your bedroom look tidy,' smiled his dad.

'Is he a Christian, like you?' Ian could have bit his tongue when he had said it, but it had just come straight out. He was trying to work it out. Tom was dead nice, really scruffy without his Batman outfit on, lived in a tip and played with kestrels for a hobby. Not at all how Ian thought religious people were. Mind you, Uncle Steve and Co. were okay most of the time. Ian wondered why his own dad always joked about the 'Bible-bashers' and the 'God-squad.'

Tom must have heard him because as he came back into the room, carrying his box, he said, 'Christian? You bet. Been rescued, you see, like this daft old bird.' He gently scooped up the kestrel and placed her in the box. 'See, I needed rescuing too. I could not do it by myself.'

Ian started to feel uncomfortable. They were on about it again. Being rescued, belonging to God. He suddenly remembered his dad's voice. 'Religion is for women and wimps. Don't forget it, son.' I won't, he thought, as he gulped a cup of thick strong tea made with evaporated milk, the worst cup of tea he had ever tasted. Don't worry, Dad, us Rathbones don't need rescuing from anything or by anyone.

It was pitch black by the time they left. The wonderful smell of rich tomato soup hit Ian as they reached the caravan. He was starving and the awful cup of tea had done nothing to stop his hunger. Over mugs of soup and crusty brown rolls stuffed with ham and salad, Ian and Dave recounted the story of the evening.

Very late a tired Ian crawled into his bunk. He remembered that he was going to keep a diary of his holiday. What a busy day to recall! By the light of his long-life batteried torch he wrote, *church, lake, skiing no good, Julia can do it (groan), kestrel, Batman Tom*. There, that should remind him. It's been a good day, he thought, if you ignore church, and tomorrow, yes tomorrow, I'll be able to ski.

But Ian was wrong. Skiing was not on the agenda for Monday at all. They got the boat out all right and then Aunt Lynda dropped the bombshell.

'Right. Ambleside, we thought. Perfect day for Ambleside.'

'Ambleside?' chorused Dave and Ian in disbelief.

'Yes. We'll take the boat to Waterhead and park it . . .'

'Moor it, Lynda,' Uncle Steve grimaced.

'Moor it there, potter round the shops. I'll buy us lunch out and then we can all walk up the Stock Ghyll Force.'

'Walk!'

'The what force?'

'It's a waterfall, and yes, the walk will do us good.'

Ian found out that once Aunt Lynda had made up her mind, that was that. Bev and Julia wanted to go shopping.

'Boy-spotting, more like it,' said Dave, eyeing the two girls who looked as if they had walked out of a magazine.

So that was that. Monday at Ambleside. No-one had told Ian that it was a long walk from the boat to the town. The shops were boring but he did buy some postcards of water-skiers and sent them to his best friends, Mark and Chris, back at home. 'You ought to see me on skis!' he wrote. Well, it was nearly the truth.

Lunch was okay. Aunt Lynda inspected about ninety restaurants before deciding that the one with pine tables and real, not plastic, plants in the window would do.

The six of them collapsed at the table. Julia had bought a giant T-shirt with 'I climbed Scafell' on it. As the nearest Julia would get to climbing the mountain was seeing it in the distance, through a car window, it was a bit of a joke. Uncle Steve embarrassed Ian by putting it on. Bev had bought some more sun-tan oil and some ghastly dangling earrings that looked like a purple bike chain.

'Order what you like,' said Aunt Lynda, so they did. Ian chose the most expensive to get his own back on her for dragging him away from the lake. Scampi and chips, followed by a large helping of blackcurrant cheesecake all washed down with two glasses of coke, put Ian in a better mood. At least for a few minutes.

Aunt Lynda stirred her coffee. She drank it black. Cuts down on the calories, she said, which was daft, Ian thought, as she had munched her way through a fresh cream trifle.

'Right . . .' Ian was beginning to dread the word. It usually meant 'wrong' as far as he was concerned. 'Stock Ghyll Force, here we come.'

'Can't I hang around here?' Ian thought it worth asking.

'Oh, no! All together, that's what I like. Come on,' and Aunt Lynda eased her well padded rear, clad in fuchsia pink jogging trousers, out of her chair.

For a middle-aged fatty, thought Ian unkindly, she can move! The pink blob was getting further away as Ian dawdled behind. It was miles to the waterfall, and uphill, and when you got there it was hardly worth the bother. Where were the thundering torrents of foamy water battering over the boulders? Aunt Lynda was a nut. This was the hottest summer for years and the mighty waterfall was a miserable trickle.

'We'll sit here and have a rest,' she commanded.

Ian lay flat on his back which was difficult on a steep hill with stones everywhere. Monday 3.30 pm. and no nearer water-skiing. Why did they not realise it was so important to him, instead of messing around playing at being tourists, sight-seeing with cameras? He would have to think of a plan to get them to go out on the lake more. But what?

It was not until later that same day that Ian started to get the germ of an idea. As he fed the germ, it grew and got hold of him. The trouble was he needed Dave's help and Dave was going to be hard to persuade.

They had got back to the boat about six. Ian had let everyone know what he thought about the matching blisters on his heels but they all ignored him. The boat had pottered off at all of five miles per hour.

'I know how you feel,' said Ian under his breath to the boat, patting the warm side of the hull. 'Sickening, isn't it? It's like getting a racehorse to give rides to kids at the school fête. Stupid. You are made for better things than this. So am I.'

At least they had a swim in the bay by the jetty. Well, he and Dave had. It was strange, there were only a few people about. Most of them brought their boats back about now and spent the evening in the hills or on the site. Ian loaded this piece of information into his computer brain making sure he pressed the 'save' button. It might come in useful.

In fact three hours later in the club, it did. They had all just shared two gigantic pizzas. Ian had to admit Aunt Lynda was great when it came to food. A singer was warbling on, much to Ian's horror. The singer was dressed to look twenty, but was much older. He wore tight black trousers with a frilled white-shirted beer-belly hanging over them. He was crooning on about 'love is all you need.' Uncle Steve and Aunt Lynda were singing along, while Bev and Julia were giggling and trying to look cool at the same time. Their attention was focused on the older teenage lads propping up the juke box, which had been turned off to accommodate the wailings of the demented singer who was now 'on his way to San José.'

Wish you were too, thought Ian, glancing out of the small paned window. Still light! Still time to be out on the boat instead of being trapped in here with all these sunburnt tired holidaymakers, making fools of themselves. That boat was wasted on this lot. Just look at today. An hour at the most, tripping down to Waterhead. An hour! And there were about eighteen hours of light in the day. It was criminal.

Mind you, if they did not want the boat, perhaps someone else could use it. Someone could borrow it and return it safely. Someone would have to make sure that everyone else was out of the way. Well nearly everyone. He would need Dave's help. They could borrow the boat, go skiing, come back and no-one would ever know. He could spend tomorrow evening on the water, not stuck in the club. Uncle Steve was just now signing up for the 'Snooker Competition, Tuesday night, Great Prizes.' The girls would go to the disco that was always on when awful singers were not. And Ian would work out what to do about Aunt Lynda. That left Dave. Ian realised that he could not drive the boat and ski at the same time. How would he persuade Dave? Ian felt braind ad. There must be a way, but he could not think of it now.

'Day on the lake,' Uncle Steve leaned over to him. 'Tomorrow, okay?'

'Sure,' Ian felt relieved. Perhaps he might not need to persuade Dave after all. He might not need to take the boat. 'All day?'

'All day. We men will put a picnic togeth r. We'll go across to what we call 'our' beach, deposit any sunbathers,' he grinned at the girls, 'and set up base camp.'

'Then we can water-ski?'

'Course, and "biscuit" '

'Biscuit?' Not food again!

'You'll have to wait and see what that is.'

'Come on, Uncle Steve, tell me.'

'No. In fact we'll "biscuit" first.'

Chapter Four

Uncle Steve was right. They 'biscuited' first, middle and last through nearly all of Tuesday. It was great fun, but it was not water-skiing.

After getting up early, Dave and Ian had been dispatched to the site shop to buy the food for the picnic. They chose sausage rolls, pickled onions, crisps, jam tarts, that later fell to pieces, an apple pie, two packets of chocolate biscuits, a bunch of bananas and a diet yoghurt for Aunt Lynda. Three bottles of pop completed their purchases and they staggered down to the boat laden with their goodies. Aunt Lynda had done, 'just a few sandwiches, in case.' Her version of a few was a whole loaf.

'Where's Uncle Steve?' Ian could see that only his uncle and Bev were missing.

'Blowing up the biscuit. They'll be here in a minute.'

Ian waited and soon they appeared, half-hidden by the biscuit. It looked like a giant inner-tube, covered in strong netting, with handles attached.

'What do you do with it?'

'Sit in it,' replied Bev. 'It's ace. We tow it behind the boat and the aim is to get whoever is in it to fall off.'

'How?'

'Well, Mum drives faster and faster and then she whirls the boat into tight circles and you bump over the wake until you fall off. You'll see.'

Sounded daft, thought Ian. As far as he was concerned the aim was to stay on. On water-skis, not fat gleaming black rubber rings. That was kids' stuff.

'Dad, can you tow me first?' Bev asked. She had come alive and actually wanted to do something on the water.

'Sure. First we'll make base camp on the other side. Then we can all have a go. All aboard.'

Six people, a giant picnic, the life jackets and an enormous inflated rubber ring take up a lot of boat, so they dawdled to the far bank of the lake. Dave and Bev leapt into the water as Mum cut the engine, and they grabbed a rope tied to the front. They wrapped it around a huge boulder and waited as the engine automatically lifted up out of the water, to avoid scraping on the lake bottom.

Marvellous! thought Ian. Twenty metres from the shore on a stationary boat. Now what?

'Everyone out!'

'Out?'

'Yes, it's quite shallow. Just take your trainers off.'

Ian obliged, tying the trainers around his neck and, thankful that he was wearing shorts, he slid over the side.

'Carry these.' Aunt Lynda passed him a blue tartan travel rug and thermos flask.

Ian wobbled his way to shore. The large flat stones under foot felt slimy and he could see his pale disembodied feet plodding along, toes splayed out to help him balance. It was really hard to grip. Too hard. With a mighty splash, Ian toppled into the cold water, getting soaked. Everyone thought it was hilarious.

'It's not funny!' he shouted, spitting water and shaking his hair.

'That's what you think!' called Dave. 'Eh, grab the rug.'

'And my coffee,' wailed Aunt Lynda, as the half-submerged thermos bobbed along the shore line.

Ian managed to retrieve it and staggered to the bank. Julia was taking more photos. He was going to look great when the holiday snaps were developed! Ian Rathbone on his stomach behind the boat and now, drenched, fully clothed. He would destroy the photos before anyone could see them. He calmed down when Dave let him wear his wet-suit, and after Aunt Lynda had forced him to drink some hot black coffee.

'Keep your trainers on, Ian,' she said kindly. 'Wear them all the time in the water. I'll buy you some more for dry land.' Ian did not mind when she leaned over and gave him a brief hug. She was okay, really.

Meanwhile Uncle Steve, Bev, Julia and Dave were back in the boat.

'You coming?' called Dave.

'Later,' Ian felt like being on his own.

'Okay. Back soon.'

Ian watched as the boat slowly manoeuvred away from the shore. With squeals that could be heard from where he was sitting, Bev got herself into the biscuit. The boat zoomed into life and Bev was dragged along, bouncing and bumping in the biscuit. Sitting up and shading his eyes from the dancing dazzling light that shimmered on the lake surface, Ian saw his uncle twist and turn the boat rapidly. Soon Bev lost her balance and soared out of the biscuit, thudding into the rocking water. He could hear the laughs as Uncle Steve turned the boat to go back for Bev. She was having a great time and had lots of turns in the biscuit before Julia and Dave did the same. I wish I had gone with them, thought Ian. It's a lot more fun than I realised. Here I am, stuck on the shore, just because I was cross at them for laughing at me. Now it will be ages before they come back and I can have a go.

'Another coffee?' offered Aunt Lynda, whose face was

rapidly turning as red as today's clothes of long scarlet shorts and sun-top.

'No thanks.'

'Why don't you explore, or something?'

'I'm okay. When will they come back?'

'When their stomachs tell them it's dinner time. Now, be a good lad and spread your clothes out to dry a bit more. Have a go at snorkelling. Dave's stuff is in the bag.'

Ian found the goggles and snorkel and edged into the lake. The water seeped into the wet-suit making him shiver but after a few moments he felt quite warm. He doggie-paddled up and down near base camp.

Here, half under the water, he could be the only person in the world. The water was very clear. He could see the individual mosses covering the stones, worn smooth by centuries of being under water. Ian dug among them and found a rusted bent spoon and what looked like a cocoa tin. As he got near a rocky outcrop, hundreds of tiny fish darted in front of him. Ian made a net shape with his fingers and gazed in fascination as the minute creatures wove in and out of his hands. The sun felt warm on his back and he had got the hang of reathing through the snorkel.

I wonder why they are all here, he thought, as the fish appeared to take no notice of him and carried on backwards and forwards for no apparent reason. And then he saw it. Soggy, off-white, like a bundle of wet clothes. Ian poked the mass and it slowly lifted, revealing a hard white object. Ian used the spoon and prodded again, harder this time and the white woolly mass rose to show a pale skull and bones.

Ian had never realised that he could move so fast as he surfaced and floundered to the shore.

'Aunt Lynda! Aunt Lynda! There's a dead thing. Look!'

Aunt Lynda shot up from the grass and hurried over. 'Where?'

'Look, by the rock outcrop.'

She stared. 'A sheep, quite often get them at the edge.'

'A sheep? But it's not big enough.'

'Decompose quickly in the water. We usually see one or two each holiday.'

'But it's awful.'

'That's life, Ian. Well death really. Things are born, live and die. Shame to end up like that, though.' She seemed very matter of fact about it.

It was just as if a cloud had gone in front of the brilliant sun. Ian shivered. 'The fish though. Lots of little ones.'

'Yes, they feed on the bits, from the sheep, you know.'

Ian had not known and now wished he didn't. He insisted on moving base camp much further along the shore. The sheep gave him the creeps and he was glad to see the others returning for lunch.

'Why have you moved?' called Uncle Steve.

Aunt Lynda glanced at Ian who looked a bit pale. Please, he thought, don't tell.

'Oh, we liked it better here. More room to spread out.' Ian decided that he would do anything, yes anything, for Aunt Lynda, for not telling them about the sheep and making him look a right wally. He soon forgot his decision though, as normality returned as he and Dave raced to eat the most bits of the crushed jam tarts.

'Fancy the biscuit?'

'Yes, Uncle Steve. Now?'

'When your dinner has gone down. Lynda, are you going to lie here all day or will you take over from Dave or Bev as observer?'

'Lie here all day.'

Uncle Steve reached out and tickled her. Ian looked away, feeling awkward. Grown-ups did not laugh and tickle each other. Not married ones. Not his mum and dad. No, he must not think about them. 'Delete,' he sent the message to his computer brain, which was not very good at deleting things Ian did not want to think about.

Eventually Aunt Lynda decided that their food would have gone down by now. At last Ian was lying across the biscuit. His bottom disappeared down the hole in the centre while his legs bent up in front of him. His hands gripped tightly onto the rubber handles on either side of him and he focused his eyes on the tow-rope harmlessly snaking out in front of him.

Everything had gone yellow. Dave had loaned him his visor. It was like the one motor-cyclists wear and covered his eyes and the top of his cheeks. It stopped the spray going into his eyes.

'Get me off, if you can,' he yelled.

'We will, don't worry!'

The engine started and the rope snake uncoiled and snapped tight. Ian felt his whole body jerk forward. As the boat kept in a straight line, he could feel the water pounding his backside and he laughed out loud at the sheer exhilaration of bumping along in the biscuit. To his amazement, he was still in it. His bottom was so firmly wedged down the hole, they would never shift him. His grip tightened. Ian was not sure if it was fear or enjoyment that made him hang on.

Help! They're turning. Lean over a bit. That's the way. Oh, no, another turn the other side. Bend quickly, Ian Rathbone, you can do it. Again! Good grief, what is Uncle Steve up to now? And another bend. Agh! He's doing a figure eight. I'll never be able to sit down again as long as I live. The waves! It's like a gale. Over the wake, once . . . twice . . . and . . .

The biscuit bounced high over the wake and Ian shot out of his hole like the top off a bottle of well-shaken pop, arched backwards over the biscuit and landed with a thud, knocking the breath from his body. He was still laughing when they returned to pick him up.

'You okay?' called his uncle.

'Great!'

'You were brill, little brother.'

'Take any photos?'

'Never thought.'

'Well, take some next time.'

'Okay.'

Ian slithered back into the biscuit, happy and aching. He could do it! Uncle Steve let him have lots of tries until he was so shattered by the combination of laughing, falling off and bombing through the water, he was too worn out to clamber back into the biscuit.

Dave heaved him aboard the boat and got ready for his turn. Ian swopped the wet-suit for Dave's boxer shorts and sat happily exhausted, while his cousin messed around in the biscuit.

'You were really good, Ian,' said Uncle Steve from his position at the steering wheel.

'Really?'

'Yes. If you can do that so well, we'll have you water-skiing in no time.'

'Now?'

'Well, I think we're running out of time. Your aunt is going to drive the boat while I biscuit and by then it will be time to pack up.'

'But you said . . . last night, you said I could ski.'

'I know, Ian, but it'll have to wait until tomorrow, I'm sorry,' Uncle Steve paused. 'Now come on, admit it, you loved the biscuit. Don't make a fuss.'

'Thought Christians always kept their promises,' muttered Ian.

'What did you say?'

'You promised, Uncle Steve.'

'Well, not really. Be reasonable. The time has gone. You've had fun. Now don't spoil everything. Tomorrow morning, you'll be first to have a go at water-skiing. Okay?'

'Okay,' replied Ian not meaning it. Tomorrow morning, eh. That's what Uncle Steve thought. This evening, more like. This evening he would take the boat and ski. Then tomorrow he could show them all. They would all be amazed, thrilled. Look at you, they would say. What an improvement! You're great, Ian.

He still had to persuade Dave to help him. That was the tricky bit. He had to get him on his own, force him, if necessary. But how? Ian kept thinking about it as the others had their turns on the biscuit and while they packed up camp and returned to the jetty. At last Ian had it partly worked out.

'Uncle Steve, me and Dave will see to the boat,' he called as they neared the jetty.

'Know what to do?'

'Stow everything, wipe down, canvas cover on, wash wet-suits.'

'All right with you, Dave?' Uncle Steve asked his son, who nodded. 'I'm leaving you responsible. You're older.'

At last Julie, Bev, Aunt Lynda and Uncle Steve disappeared up the path to the caravan. Now for it.

'Dave.'

'Yea.'

'Got to talk.'

'What about? Here, help with these jackets.'

'Just shut up a minute. Listen.'

'Hurry up. What are you on about?'

'Dave, you've got to help me.'

'Do what?'

'Ski.'

'Course, tomorrow.'

'No, not tomorrow. Tonight. This evening.'

'This evening! Don't be daft.'

'I'm deadly serious.' Ian sat opposite his cousin, staring into his eyes. 'We borrow the boat, while they're all at the club. After tea. They'll never know. You drive. I ski. Get it?' Ian paused. What would Dave say?

Chapter Five

Dave said nothing. He stared at his cousin who was inches away from him. Ian could almost feel the silence. The only sound that penetrated his mind was the soft lub-lub of the water as the moored boat rocked up and down. Eventually Dave spoke.

'You must be mad.'

'I'm not. You've got to help me.'

'Got to?'

'Yes.' This was more difficult than Ian had thought. 'I've got to learn to ski. I'll never do it at this rate. It's Tuesday already and Mum and Dad fetch us on Saturday. I know I could do it, if only I could get a long time at it. It's hopeless when we're all together, in and out of the boat and the wet-suit, just a few tries.' Ian paused. 'Look, all I want you to do is to drive the stupid thing. You can drive it, can't you?'

'Course. It's simple. But I'm not allowed.'

'Not allowed! Are you a wimp, or something?'

'No.' Dave started to stand up, but Ian pushed him back onto the seat. 'It's against the rules. I'm too young to drive alone. You've got to be at least sixteen.'

Ian ignored that bit. 'But you do know how to do it?'

'I told you, yes. I've watched Dad and Mum enough, and steered myself. But I'm not doing it.'

'You look sixteen . . .'

'Come off it. I'm shorter than you.'

'Well, sit on a cushion or something. Put your Dad's sailor hat on. No one will see us anyway.'

'You're right. No one will see us. 'Cos we're not going.' Dave spoke slowly and deliberately. He folded his arms. A battle was raging inside him. Oh, he could drive the boat but it was wrong, really wrong, to take it and do what Ian suggested. His dad would go bananas, he might bang the boat getting past the jetty, and anyway all the time this little voice was saying, 'Don't do it, Dave. Don't do it.' He sighed as another thought popped into his head.

'You can't ski without an observer.'

'Rubbish.'

'Look, I ought to know. One to drive, one to ski and someone to observe.'

'Observe what?'

'Well, make sure the tow-rope doesn't get tangled up. Watch the skier to see he is safe and to know when he falls off. Why do you think there are always a few of us in the boat, dummy?'

'Dummy yourself. You drive and observe. Just turn your head round while you are driving.'

'But someone will see. They'll report us to the wardens.'

A gleam came into Ian's eyes. Report *us* to the wardens, Dave had said. Us. Ian was half way there. If he kept shooting Dave's objections down, he could get his cousin to agree.

'Look,' he said. 'There's hardly anyone about. By the time we all go to the club there will be no-one around. No-one will see us. Get it? No-one will know if we are twelve or sixty, or if we've got an observer, because no-one will see us.'

Dave looked thoughtful. It was true that the lakeside would be deserted soon.

'Other boats might see us.'

'Come off it. They will be too far away.'

Dave tried once more. 'It's stealing. Stealing is wrong.'

'Stealing!' Ian had had enough. 'Who does the boat belong to? Your dad! You are borrowing it, not stealing. Borrowing, dumb-brain.'

'He'd never let us borrow it, if we asked him.'

'But we aren't going to ask him.' Ian was nearly screeching by now. 'That's the whole point. We borrow it, put it back and he won't ever know.'

'I can't. It's wrong.' Dave felt steam-rollered by his cousin's persistence.

'Listen. You can. If you don't do this, Dave, you're the biggest weak-kneed, girlish coward I've ever met. You've got the guts of a jelly and the nerve of a dead parrot. You Christians are all the same. Church and being nice but no, no . . .' Ian just stopped himself from swearing, 'no guts!'

He had hit a sore point inside Dave who smothered the little voice saying 'Don't do it,' and jumped up.

'Guts! I'll show you who's got guts, Ian Rathbone. I've got more guts in my little finger,' he waved it aloft, 'than you've got in the whole of your body. We'll borrow the boat, you can ski till you drop and I'll prove to you I've got guts.'

He leaped on his cousin and they tumbled onto the narrow floor of the boat locked in mortal combat. Dave was just about to thin Ian's wild hair by pulling a handful out, when a shadow fell across them.

'What's going on here?' shouted Uncle Steve, although it was pretty obvious.

'Just playing,' called Ian from somewhere under Dave. 'You say a word,' he hissed into his cousin's ear, 'and I'll kill you.'

'It's tea-time. I leave you in charge and you've done nothing at all.' He yanked his son up by the seat of his pants. 'Nothing. You two couldn't be responsible for falling out of bed!' Uncle Steve continued to lecture them, while they tidied everything away. On and on he went, until Dave and Ian forgot their quarrel and got the giggles.

'Sorry, Dad, it won't happen again.'

'Too right it won't. Dave, I expected more of you. You know what to do and I trusted you.' Dave felt as if he had been winded. Trust you! When he was going to borrow, no steal, the boat in an hour's time! He couldn't go through with it. Then he caught the look on Ian's face. He would have to do it, but not for long.

The boys set off up the path to the caravan out of Uncle Steve's earshot.

'Right, I've got it all worked out, Dave.'

'How?'

'Just do as I say, when I say. It's easy. Act normal,' Ian paused. 'Hello, Aunt Lynda,' he smiled angelically, 'sorry we're late. We were messing about. Oh, goody, meat pies,' and the family attacked the meal with their customary enthusiasm.

Julia and Bev disappeared to get ready for the club disco. Uncle Steve obviously fancied his chances in the snooker competition as he went so far as to put on a white shirt and tie.

'What are you doing, Lynda?'

'I'll tidy up a bit and then go to the disco with the girls.' The girls heard and a joint groan came out of their room. 'It's okay,' called Aunt Lynda, 'I'll sit at the edge. I won't cramp your style.' She turned to Dave and Ian. 'Are you boys going to watch the snooker?' They nodded. 'Best hurry up then, Steve Davis here is raring to go.'

It was a competition where each player had to play several games. Uncle Steve was quite good and would probably make it to the semi-finals, at least. Ian and

Dave hung around with him, in the snooker room, next to the club, for about half an hour.

'Uncle Steve,' Ian asked very politely. 'Do you mind if me and Dave go next door to the disco? It's a bit boring in here.'

'If you like. Seen some nice girls?' he teased.

Ian blushed. 'I like listening to the music. Better than that singer, anyway!'

'See you later then. Bye,' and Uncle Steve returned his attention to the game.

'Right, this is it.' Ian grabbed Dave's arm and they made their way out of the entertainment complex. 'We'll fetch the wet-suit.'

'Can't. Look,' Dave pointed. His mum could be clearly seen inside the caravan watching television. 'She hasn't gone yet.'

'Never mind, we'll manage without.'

They ran to the boat, passing holidaymakers who were dressed for an evening out, but who all sported red or peeling faces. As Ian had predicted there was no-one at the jetty, only the swan on his beat, up and down. They eventually got the boat uncovered.

'The key!' exclaimed Dave.

'I told you, leave it to me.' Ian pulled the key out of his pocket. It was attached to a globe of cork so it would float if dropped into the water. 'Borrowed it off your dad when he was getting changed in the caravan.'

Dave started the engine, put his dad's hat on and slowly eased the boat out of its mooring. He felt a strange mix inside. Now that the adventure had started, he was mostly excited but deep down inside him was a little hole that was worrying away. Fortunately the hole disappeared as he threaded the boat through the islands and past the six mile per hour limit. She handled like a dream. All this power at his fingertips.

'Hold on, Ian.' He opened the throttle and they were

flying, laughing as the boat cut across the lake, the wake creaming behind them. Cutting the engine Dave said, 'This is where you get out. Ready?'

Ian looked around him. A few speed boats in the distance, the lake calm, the sky still pure blue and the sun a golden ball, heading out towards the far hills. Perfect. With much puffing and heaving they got the skis, tow-rope and buoyancy jackets out. Ian stripped off his jumper and jeans and put the buoyancy jacket on over his T-shirt and swimming trunks. It felt surprisingly cold for such a nice day. Shame he had not got the wet-suit.

At last Ian was in the water. It was freezing and great goose-pimples erupted all over his body. Ian didn't care. He was concentrating on the skiing.

'Just a few goes,' called Dave, standing at the back of the boat slowly threading the tow-rope out, so it would not catch on the engine. He would never be able to drive and observe at the same time. Easiest to assume that Ian would fall over and zoom the boat for a few seconds before stopping.

'Ready?'

'Sure.'

Once again the black engine vibrated with life and Ian experienced the sudden force on his arms and legs. Once again he fell over into the stinging water. He now had reddened goose-pimples but at least he had kept the skis on.

As he waited for the boat to circle round for him, Ian noticed darkening shadows creeping down the hillsides. Little fluffy clouds were appearing in the sky, scattered haphazardly about. Each one was fringed in shimmering pink and gold as the lowering sun's rays lit them up. It was beautiful.

Ian had plenty of time to watch the sky. He kept falling over and spent most of the time lying in Lake

Windermere waiting for Dave to bring the boat round for him. What he did not notice was that the puffs of cloud were getting steadily darker as the sun dropped closer to the mountain that Dave said was Coniston Old Man.

'Last time.'

'No, Dave. Two more.'

'Okay!'

This time Ian was up, very briefly, but up. Dave had stopped the boat quickly, as usual, and Ian was furious.

'Observe, you idiot,' he yelled, as Dave came close to him. 'I was up and you stopped. Keep going. Understand?'

'Okay.' I'll keep going, thought Dave. He will just have to sit there for ages until I come back for him. 'Very last time.'

'If you say so.'

'I do.'

Ian braced himself and with an exhilarating rush his body lifted up out of the water . . . and out a bit more . . . and over he went. Splat. He sighed as the boat accelerated further away from him. 'Stop, you moron!' he called, but the boat kept going, growing gradually smaller. Ian was beginning to see why observers were the rule. He'd give that Dave a piece of his mind when he came back to pick him up.

He could see the boat slow down and he waited, lying on his back, feet still in the skis, for Dave to return. He waited . . . and waited.

'Turn the boat,' he yelled, but Dave was too far away to hear anything. 'Come on, stop messing about.'

But Dave was not messing about. He had wanted to keep Ian hanging around but not like this. He tried again and again to restart the rocking blue and white craft. Nothing. Nothing at all. Not a gurgle, a cough or a splutter.

Panic flooded over Dave like a wave crashing down upon him. It would not go. He could not start it. He sat down and buried his head in his hands, clutching his spray damped curls so tightly it hurt. Might help him to concentrate.

Why won't you go, he thought, kicking the panel in front of him. Slowly a thought stole into his reluctant mind. No, it couldn't be! Surely not! Ian had said that he had thought of everything. But the petrol! Had he remembered that? Dave thought back. Dad had filled up early that morning. Dave could visualise the petrol and shots of oil glugging through the clear plastic pipes from the pump at the marina. The pungent smell came back to him, strong and overpowering. All day they had biscuited and Dave knew only too well how much fuel the Cobra used. Cost them a fortune each holiday. He looked at the gauge which did not help. It showed nothing unless the engine was on. And that was the whole point. It was not on. It would not come on.

He looked around. The lake was so big and his powerless boat so small. He was a long way from the bank. It was getting colder so he put Ian's jumper on top of his own and sat down to wait, but he did not know what for. Only one person could help him.

'Oh, God,' he cried out loud, 'I'm sorry. I knew we shouldn't take the boat. I knew it was wrong. I've let you down. Let Dad and Mum down. Please, please, will you help me?' Dave stopped suddenly. Help him! What about Ian? Wherever was he?

Dave stood up and stared across the rippling lake. He could see nothing. Just a couple of distant boats returning to safe moorings. No sign of Ian. The more he looked, the less he could see.

'He'll be hidden in the waves,' Dave said aloud, to convince himself. 'He'll be okay. The buoyancy jacket will keep him up . . .' He turned his words back to God.

'Please help Ian. I know he doesn't believe in you, but don't hold that against him. He's my friend. Please help him. Get us rescued. Please.'

Sitting down he prayed 'please help us' over and over again. He felt so helpless, and it was all his fault. He was the oldest. He should have known better. What had he said? 'I'll show you who has got guts!' Well his guts had gone when the engine died.

In alarm Dave noticed that the boat was slowly drifting towards Ambleside. He could see the twinkling lights of Waterhead Pier ahead and the thought struck him that it would soon be dark.

The thought struck Ian too. The fantastic sunset was fading and the sun had nestled behind the mountains. Immediately Ian felt even colder. His T-shirt clung to him limply as he struggled to remove the skis. Lose them as well and goodness knew what would happen. He could hear no sound from the boat. He could hardly glimpse it as he rocked up and down clutching the wooden skis for support and grateful for his buoyancy jacket.

The boat's not coming, he thought. It's not coming! Not coming! Fear threatened to engulf him. He breathed deeply. 'Don't panic,' he said aloud. 'Don't panic! It'll be all right. It will.'

But would it? How could it? There was no escaping the facts. Ian Rathbone was alone, in the middle of a lake, bobbing up and down, so cold he felt as if his feet had dropped off, holding on to wooden skis, with only a jacket to keep him afloat. He was frozen, it was getting dark, there were no other boats in sight. Ian gulped as tears started to run down his face. He was absolutely terrified.

Chapter Six

Purple fingers of colour smudged across the slowly darkening sky and the hillsides seemed to fade away, so that it was hard to tell what was hill or grass or trees.

Ian could not have been further from the bank if he had tried and he could hardly see the boat now. It was even further away than the shore. There was only one thing for it. He would have to swim. It looked about half a mile to the eastern shore, which was where the caravan site was. Half a mile. That was about thirty lengths of the swimming baths back home. Thirty lengths equalled, let's see, about half an hour. At home he could do a length in much less than a minute, so it would not take him much longer here.

He set off, leaning on the skis, with his legs kicking up and down, like in front crawl. The skis kept twisting round and Ian constantly wrestled with them, so he could keep pointing in the right direction. On and on he kicked, his leaden legs automatically moving, his chin resting on the skis. After what seemed like hours, Ian trod water and looked around.

It was hopeless. The shore was no nearer. He would never make it. Looking up, Ian saw that the sky was not much darker. That was it. He could not tell the time in the water. He would count. One and two and . . . slowly and surely. He would count the seconds and after five minutes he would look and see how far he had come.

One and two and . . . come on, Ian, you can do it . . . and kick and push . . . and nineteen and twenty and . . . keep going, got to do this at least thirty times a minute . . . and fifty-nine and sixty and back to one and two and . . .

Ian's breath came in huge gasps. He had stopped shivering by now as the exertion had warmed him up. He lost count of how much lake he swallowed, hating the sour taste that lingered in his mouth.

At last five minutes were up. He stopped. It was hopeless. He did not seem to be moving at all. It would take him all night to reach the shore. As he rested the water tugged at his legs, trying to move him around. Perhaps that was the answer? Perhaps he could let the currents float him along anywhere. But where was anywhere? The lake was not like the sea where the incoming tide would land him on the beach. These currents were mean and nasty. They would just drag him up and down the middle of the lake.

Just then something soft brushed past his left leg. Ian was galvanised into motion and set off like a rocket. An eel! Metres long, ready to wrap itself around his legs. Can't be, said one part of his brain. They live much nearer the bottom, but that did not stop Ian imagining the thick long twisted bodies chasing him through the shadowed water.

What else had Dave said, or was it Bev? Pike with teeth like crocodiles! Ian was not in Lake Windermere now. This was an infested tropical swamp. He was an explorer weighed down by back-pack, not skis, chased by crocodiles with gaping jaws ready to demolish him, bite by bite. In his terror, Ian swam faster and faster. He could hear them coming, feel the ripples of water as their iron-clad bodies thrashed after him. They were getting closer, closer . . . it was no good . . . they were almost upon him. Ian screamed, a long inhuman cry as it got him.

The piece of gnarled driftwood gently brushed past his body and harmlessly continued on its aimless journey.

Ian stopped. Chest heaving, heart racing, he brought himself carefully back to reality. Driftwood not crocodile. Lake District not jungle. Mum always said that he watched too much television and it was no good for him.

He could ignore it no longer. It was nearly dark and he did not like it. Getting dark was fun when you wanted to stay up late, or were rescuing a kestrel, or drinking tea in Tom Fraser's cluttered kitchen. Getting dark when you were alone in the middle of a lake was no fun at all. It was awful.

Ian slowly resumed his kicking, getting more tired with each stroke. He would never make it. He would have to stay out here all night, aimlessly swimming. Someone would find him tomorrow. They would see his buoyancy jacket. They were sure to.

But it might be too late. Tomorrow. It would be at least twelve hours before the lake was alive with people and boats. And would he be alive then? He would never last the night.

I'll either freeze to death, he thought, gazing at the purple and green blotches that covered the bumpy carpet of goose-pimples on his hands and arms, or I'll fall asleep and slip out of this jacket.

They'll never find me. I'll fall to the bottom of the deep, deep lake and lie there. The pike will attack me and little fish will thrive on bits of my body. He shuddered and felt sick as the vision of the decomposing sheep swam into his mind. That's what I'll be like. Perhaps they'll find my T-shirt washed up on shore or maybe a floating ski. I'm never going to leave this lake.

In his fear and panic, Ian started to imagine his funeral. Would anybody cry? And how do you have a funeral if you don't find the body? Perhaps they would bring one of those round things of flowers and throw it on the water, like when they buried people at sea. Perhaps they would put a bit in the paper about him. 'Ian Rathbone, lost at sea, no, lake.' Julia would have his computer, Mum would never moan about the state of his bedroom again and he would never learn to water-ski. Dad and Aunt Lynda would probably have another one of their noisy discussions about God and things.

He remembered Aunt Lynda and the dead sheep, 'Things are born, live and die. Shame to end up like that though.'

'I don't want to die,' he called out loud, startling himself by the sound of his own voice. 'I want to live.'

He had no energy left. He just lay there, letting the water take him where it wanted. He must stay awake until he was rescued.

His tired brain woke up. Rescued. That was it. He needed to be rescued. But how? By whom? By Dave? But where was Dave? Where was the boat? Why hadn't Dave come to the rescue? Only Dave knew where he was. Only Dave? Was that true? What about Dave's God? The Son of Man . . . what was it . . . seeking and saving . . . something . . . the lost. That was it. Seek and save the lost. Well, he was lost all right, and he needed finding and saving.

From deep within his despair something started to take shape. A thought grew. He would see if this Son of Man could seek him, but he was not sure how to go about it. He would have to ask him, and Ian was not even convinced that he existed, let alone if he could help him.

Uncle Steve and Co. talked to God at all sorts of funny times. So he would do that. He would talk to God.

'Hello,' he hesitated. 'Hello, God,' Ian's voice sounded thin and weary. 'Can you help me? I'm lost. I need seeking, like the Son of Man does. Can you seek me?

I'm somewhere in the north end of Lake Windermere, in the Lake District in England, if that's any help.' He paused. 'And if you can find me, can you save me, get me rescued, please. I don't want to die.'

Could he do it? Ian was not sure. It would soon be very dark. Could God see a very cold and wet boy in a big lake in the dark? And if he could, what would he do about it? Ian didn't know, but it was his last hope, his very last hope.

Dave was also on his last hope. He'd prayed and prayed and tried to keep warm. He felt scared but knew that he would be okay as he had the boat to protect him. As long as there was not a storm, he would be fine. Over to the west a light wind moaned softly through the woods and Dave tried to shut the sound out of his ears. It was too much like the ghostly Crier of Claife, out to claim another ferryman.

It's just a story, he told himself, there's no such thing as ghosts, but it was hard to believe that alone in the rocking boat.

He fiddled about in the boat, poking under the cold, clammy seats, hunting through the dashboard cupboards. Unearthing a bar of chocolate, he rammed it into his mouth, heedless of the sticky brown trickles oozing down his chin. At least he felt a bit better now. Dave's hand closed over a funny shaped object right at the back of a cupboard. A torch? He examined it. Not a torch but something a whole lot better. A flare. When Dad first bought the boat, he had got the flares, in case they were ever marooned. You set it off and a great arc of light shot up into the sky. They had tried them out. The flares made bonfire night fireworks look tame.

He would set off the flare. Someone would see it and rescue him. Rescue Ian, more importantly. But if they were rescued, then they would be found out. They would be in terrible trouble. He would have to do it, trouble or not. They had got to be rescued.

Dave stood, legs apart to keep his balance, held the flare in his hand and set it off. A great sparkling ball of red set the night on fire, lighting up the boat and a vast area of lake.

Ian saw it, feeling its glow on his face. Hope grew inside him. Someone must see it. They must.

He was right. A lot of people did, people who had been discussing the whereabouts of a certain Dave and Ian.

The super snooker star, Uncle Steve, had not been so super after all. Knocked out of the competition in the quarter finals by a 'fluke shot, if ever I saw one,' he had then gone into the club to join his wife.

'Are they enjoying themselves?' he asked.

'Julia and Bev have been dancing all the time.' Aunt Lynda replied, pointing to a bunch of gyrating arms and legs. 'Over there.'

'And the boys?'

'What boys?'

'Dave and Ian,' he grinned. 'Can't forget those two.'

'Aren't they with you?'

'They were. Got bored and came in here a good hour and half ago.'

Aunt Lynda looked at him. 'Little monkeys, they never did.'

'I'll go and look for them, Lynda.'

'Try the arcade. That Ian loves video games.'

Uncle Steve tried the arcade, the chip shop, the snooker room, the gents' loos, and the caravan, before returning.

'I can't find them,' he said, sitting down crossly. 'They wouldn't have gone into town, would they?'

'What for? Look at the trouble we had dragging them round Ambleside. No attraction in town for those two.'

Uncle Steve asked the girls but they had no idea where they were.

'Aunt Lynda,' said Julia slowly. 'Ian's awfully keen on the boat.'

'He wouldn't . . . no, they couldn't . . .' Aunt Lynda was all flustered.

'Sit down, Lynda. I'll just run down to the jetty. They're probably feeding the ducks.'

But the ducks were all asleep, heads tucked beneath their wings, as if they had been chopped off. The jetty was deserted. So were the Cobra's moorings.

'The little . . . the stupid . . .' Uncle Steve, for once, was lost for words. He stared hard up the lake but could see only moored boats and the dark blobs of the islands. The lake bent out of view and he ran back to the club.

'They've taken the boat . . . it's gone,' he panted. 'The stupid idiots.'

'Perhaps someone else has taken it?' suggested Bev hopefully.

'Do you really think so?' Uncle Steve shook his head. 'We'll have to get up a search party.' He moved among the tables quietly talking to the regular holidaymakers that he knew well. An assorted group, mainly men, got up and followed him, while some of the women clustered around Aunt Lynda.

'What if they get into trouble? Out there, all alone,' she said.

'Mum,' said Bev. 'They're nearly thirteen. Stop worrying. I'll go with Dad.' She turned to Julia. 'Take Mum back to the caravan. Get her to make a load of food. That'll calm her down.'

Bev ran to the caravan, grabbed a pile of towels, two anoraks and her trainers and ran down to the jetty. Just in time. She leaped into Jim Norris' boat, where Dad was, and joined the little armada of craft that headed across the blackened water.

'I've told them to search the north side of the lake. That's where they always like to go – our beach, the skiing area. I just hope we find them before it's pitch black.' He bowed his head. Bev reached over and squeezed his hand as she silently joined him in asking God to help them find the boys. She felt anxious but knew that they would be safe as long as they stayed in the boat. But what if they had capsized it? What if they had tried to be clever and done a tight turn too fast? What if Dave and Ian were drowned already?

Dad, Bev and Jim Norris cruised slowly, as did all the other boats, each person scanning the choppy water, looking for the boat hidden in its folds.

'Look!' the joint cry from the boats shattered the air, as a red ball lit up the sky.

'The flare! Thank God they've had the sense to set off the flare!' and Jim Norris speeded up his boat as they headed up the lake.

Bev let her breath out slowly. The flare meant the boys were safe, at least sort of. They must be in the boat to set the flare off. But they must be in trouble as well, otherwise they would have returned ages ago.

After a few minutes, they approached the Cobra and slowed down. Bev could see the stick figure of one of the boys waving as they drew close. Thank God, everything was all right. Jim Norris brought his boat alongside and all but two of the others returned to the jetty, the crisis over. Or so they thought.

Chapter Seven

Dave looked at his father. 'Sorry, Dad,' he muttered.

'Sorry! You will be,' said his dad, leaping aboard.
'What's the problem?'

'No petrol . . . but Dad . . .'

'Can you give us a tow?' Dad asked Jim, who nodded.
'But Dad . . .'

'Silly boys, ran out of fuel. Would you believe it?'

'Dad!' Dave screeched. 'Dad, I've lost Ian.'

At last he had his father's full attention.

'Lost Ian?' He peered into the boat, expecting to see
his nephew emerge from the front. 'Lost Ian?'

'We were water-skiing . . .'

'You were *what*?' His dad cried, not believing what
he heard.

'Well Ian was skiing. He fell off. The boat stopped.'

'Where is he?'

'I don't know. Oh, Dad, he'll be okay, won't he?'

There was no reply. 'How long ago?'

'I don't know. The sun was just going down.'

'About an hour! Here, Jim,' he called. 'Ian's in the
water, somewhere. Get the others. Bev, get in here!'

Jim roared off and after a seeming age returned with
the flotilla of boats, their lights blazing.

'Right,' said Dad, 'Bev, stay here with Dave. Let's
search.'

'I've radioed the warden and police,' said Jim. 'Their

boats have got stronger lights.'

The police! thought Dave. He would be locked up after this. He sat wrapped up in the anoraks on the drifting Cobra. Bev put her arm around him and he felt strangely comforted.

'If he dies, it'll be my fault,' Dave sobbed. Seeing all the rescue boats criss-crossing the lake, their lights cutting paths through the darkness, had made him realise how serious Ian's situation was.

'They'll find him,' Bev tried to reassure him. 'We've prayed like mad. Bet you have too.'

Dave nodded. 'But it's so big and dark and cold. He'll be terrified, Bev. He thinks he has guts but he hasn't; no more than me.'

'We'll just have to wait. Come on, be brave,' and she sat even closer to him.

Meanwhile Ian still floated in his buoyancy jacket. He had lost his grip on the skiis and they had disappeared. He watched the boats and the lights. Surely they would find him soon. He could not stay awake much longer.

Lights blazed a route near to him.

'Here,' he called, waving with what was left of his strength. But his cries were lost, rubbed out by the sound of the engine. Ian was too tired now to bother. He did not feel panic or fear. He was just waiting for his fate, whatever that might be. The water was getting choppier, churned up by the wakes of the boats. A foaming wake smacked him in the face, sending him reeling. He could not last much longer. It would soon be over.

Suddenly a blinding light caught his face and he screwed up his eyes as the beam held him fiercely in its grip. He could not see, everything was white inside the secret world of his eyelids. He was floating, fading away into this tunnel of glaring brightness.

Something fastened on his arms and pulled, but Ian lay there like a sodden weight.

'Hold on, Ian! Hold on!' The words did not make sense.

Something hooked the back of his jacket and dragged him along. Barely opening his eyes and squinting into the terrible glare, Ian saw a huge dark shape, like a whale, looming over him. It was better to keep his eyes shut.

'He's too weak. Ian, heave yourself up the swim ladder.'

Swim ladder? His fuddled brain was like a blank computer screen.

Something splashed into the water next to him. 'It's okay, Ian, I've got you.' Big powerful arms heaved him onto the ladder while others reached down and dragged him over the side of the large boat, landing him like an over-sized fish in a heap on the bottom of the boat.

Someone wrapped him up. Rolls of material enveloped him and Ian could feel the water pour off his body onto the floor. He just lay there.

'Ian, you're safe. Can you hear me?'

He tried to speak, but could only croak.

'We'll soon be back on dry land.'

'Dave?'

'Your friend? He's fine. Your uncle's with him.'

'He saved me.'

'Your uncle? Yes, he got us all organised.'

'No. The Son of Man.'

'Son of man?' The boatman was puzzled, but Ian was too exhausted to talk any more. 'Send the signal,' the boatman called to the driver. 'I think he's going delirious. Then hurry up!'

Hooters sounded, lights flashed and the boats turned back to the jetty, in a V formation, all following the rescuer's boat, escorted by the police and warden.

Half the occupants of the caravan site were waiting at the jetty.

'Must go to the cottage hospital.'

'Better off in his own bed.'

'Boys!'

'Well, whatever will they think of next!'

Aunt Lynda appeared. She had recovered from her shock and was bossing everyone about.

'Up to bed with Ian. Steve and Jim, will you carry him? Dave are you okay to walk?' In an emergency Aunt Lynda was at her best. 'Put him down,' she commanded. Ian was plopped, like a sausage roll, onto the caravan floor, unrolled from his blankets, completely stripped by his aunt, rubbed all over with a hairy towel and carried into his aunt and uncle's double bed. Two jumpers and hiking socks were forced over his pyjamas and he was buried under a mountain of blankets.

'Drink this.' Obediently Ian swallowed the hot sweetened brandy, coughed and choked, and gratefully followed it with a mug of drinking chocolate. At last he had stopped shivering. The noise from all the people crammed into the caravan faded abruptly and Ian fell fast asleep, too tired to even consider what might happen in the morning.

Dave was so relieved that his greeny-blue cousin was alive that he did not mind taking second place in the fuss and attention.

Plied with sandwiches, he told and retold his story to his mum, dad, Bev and Julia and the remains of the rescuers, who were enjoying the rest of Ian's medicinal brandy and Aunt Lynda's fruit cake.

So far no-one had gone mad at him. So far. He had the distinct impression that would wait and he was in no hurry to find out exactly what it would involve.

The rescuers finally went, still chattering into the clear night air. It was very late.

'Thank goodness, that's over,' sighed Uncle Steve, collapsing into a dishevelled heap on the padded bench.

'Thank God, more likely.' Aunt Lynda spoke quietly.

Dave looked at her. She had gone from being all efficient and ordering everyone around, to crumpling up. Her face sagged and the jolly smile she had put on while the rescuers demolished their supper, had disappeared. Dave moved over to her, where she was pottering aimlessly in the kitchen area.

'Mum, I'm sorry. Really.' He put his arms around her waist. 'I won't do it again.'

'You can say that again,' his dad interrupted.

'Steve, leave it tonight. I've had enough.' She turned to look at her son. 'We were worried sick, but I don't suppose you need me to tell you how stupid you have been.'

'No, Mum.'

'Well, all's well that ends well.' She sat down, leaving the dishes unwashed in the sink. 'Why don't we all pray and thank God together, then go to bed. I'm shattered.'

Julia listened as her cousins, uncle and aunt all thanked God for helping them to find the boys. It was really odd but she wanted to join in. Tonight she had seen a different side of being a Christian. She knew that they had all asked God to rescue the boys but that had not made them sit around waiting for Dave and Ian to materialise out of thin air. No, they had organised a search. Aunt Lynda had worried like any mum would, and Julia was still waiting for Uncle Steve to tell the boys off. Strange that he had not. Her dad would have been yelling for weeks! And Bev! That had been a surprise! Making sure that her mum was okay and then off like a shot to join in the search in her best black party dress, that was now ruined. Bev, who usually went through life at one mile an hour so as not to spoil her hair or make-up. It was all confusing. They were all ordinary, but different somehow and it seemed to be something to do with God.

Julia's thoughts were interrupted as Bev prayed; 'Dear God, thank you that Dave and Ian were rescued. Please help Ian not to get ill, pneumonia or something. Thank you for all the people who helped in the rescue . . .'

Dave keeled over, fast asleep.

'Let's leave him there. I'll get a blanket.' Aunt Lynda went into Dave's room and came out grinning.

'Looks like me and you are in the bunks tonight, Steve. I haven't been in a sleeping bag for years.'

'Well, I'm having the top one,' said Uncle Steve, in a whining voice, like a spoilt child.

'Not fair!'

'Come off it, Lynda. You'll plummet through it.'

'You cheeky so and so. Calling me heavy, are you?'

'Cuddly, that's all.' And Uncle Steve hugged her, making her giggle.

At about eleven o'clock, Dave stirred into life. He had slept through breakfast being made around him, and the stream of visitors who kept popping up to make sure that the boys were well. As he opened his eyes he caught Dad looking at him so he shut them again quickly. He had still got Dad to face. He had not fooled him though.

'Morning, Dave,' Dad boomed. 'Feel like a boat trip?'

Dave grimaced, wondering what was coming next. Dad leaned across and tickled him, right in the stomach, where it half tickles and half hurts. Dave squirmed about, fighting his way out of the blankets. He was surprised to find himself fully dressed. That would save one job today.

'Here, sit still. Toast okay this morning? We've run out of cereal again.'

'Three pieces. Loads of marmalade.' Dave paused. 'Where's Mum?'

'She's taken Julia and Bev out in the car. Market day somewhere. They've gone bargain hunting. I've got to stay here as jailor.'

'Jailor?'

'Keep you two prisoners under lock and key.' Dave looked away as his dad continued to talk, burning the toast in the process. He ate the burnt bits himself and made some more for Dave. 'What do you think we should do with you?' Silence. 'Did you hear?'

'Yes, Dad.'

'Well then?'

'Don't know.'

'Don't know! Well, what would you do if you were me?' Go bananas, thought Dave, but that wasn't Dad's style. Usually it was a lecture, or no pocket money or television. But pinching the boat, being rescued by half the population of Windermere, calling in the warden and police, hardly came into the usual bracket. Dave just munched his toast. Dad made some more.

'Well, Dave, I'm not going to do anything.'

'Not do anything?' Dave echoed in disbelief.

'That's right.' his dad hesitated. 'Tell me, how did it feel last night? I know what happened, you told us enough yesterday. But how did you feel?'

It was such a relief to talk that the words poured out of Dave like water from a tap. 'Oh, Dad, it was awful. I knew all along that it was wrong, but it was exciting as well. But when I lost Ian, you know the petrol running out, I thought he would drown, and I was so frightened. I waited and waited. It was horrible . . . horrible . . . and then you came . . .'

Dad nodded. 'That's what I thought. Horrible. It must have been very frightening for you both. So, Dave, that is why there is going to be no further punishment, you understand?'

Dave nodded. The pair of them looked like matching

statues, with just their heads going up and down.

'Well, just one punishment. You've got to finish off the toast,' and Dad laughed. Dave felt so loved, so safe and secure that he burst into tears which made him feel very silly. He felt a right wally crying because Dad had been nice to him. He had not even cried, well not much, when he was lost on the boat. Dad took charge.

'Right, blow nose, have shower, wash up mess.'

'Right, Dad.'

'And then we will see if your partner in crime has woken up from his beauty sleep.'

'Take more than sleep to make him beautiful!' Dave went thoughtful. 'Dad, are you going to be mad with Ian, 'cos it was more my fault than his?'

'No, Dave, I'll treat him the same as you. He must have been terrified out of his wits. I'm just glad that he's safe. Now hurry up and we'll check if he is okay.'

Dave eventually got showered and dressed and then went with his dad to the bedroom door to see how Ian was.

'Ian,' Uncle Steve knocked. 'Are you awake yet? Are you okay?'

There was silence so Uncle Steve gently opened the door to see a mound of bedding topped by a sunburnt face and sun bleached hair. Two big blue eyes stared at him, scared stiff. He was really in for it now.

Chapter Eight

Ian thought he was more scared now than when he had been in the lake. But that was because the lake was last night, and this was now – 12.27 by his watch.

He had been awake for ages, kicking off some of the extra covers and struggling out of the two jumpers and hiking socks. He was boiling hot and dying for the loo, but he had not dared leave the safe haven of the bed, in case Uncle Steve saw him.

Their voices had mumbled away from the other end of the caravan and Ian was sure that he had heard Dave sobbing. Whatever Uncle Steve had done, it must be awful if Dave had cried. Well, he, Ian, would not cry, whatever happened. Even if he got belted, like when Dad had walloped him one when he had broken the kitchen window by throwing his revolting dinner at it. Steamed fish, it had been, and the white sticky goo had run down the wall, chased by the bullet green peas. He hadn't meant the plate to go through the glass. He had only intended to skim the whole revolting mess into the sink. It wasn't his fault he was such a bad shot.

Anyway perhaps he wouldn't get a belting. Maybe it would be a yelling, like his mum was good at. Ian was so used to it, he took no notice. But Ian could never remember Uncle Steve bawling his head off. Well, only once. And that was when they watched his team lose the F.A. Cup Final at Wembley on television. Half the street must have heard him that day. So, if he wasn't going to get belted or yelled at, what was Uncle Steve going to do that was so bad it made his cousin cry? Ian couldn't imagine, but he just hoped that it would be over soon.

Uncle Steve squeezed into the room and plonked himself on the bed.

'Afternoon, Ian,' he smiled. 'How are you feeling?'

'Hot.' Ian was suspicious of his uncle's friendliness.

'No wonder. Its about seventy seven degrees out there,' he pointed through the window, 'and about a hundred and twenty in here.' He threw back the covers and instinctively Ian curled up in a ball.

'Stomach ache?'

'No, need the loo.' Ian got up and made a run for it. In the safety of the bathroom he dealt with his most urgent need, and then sat on the floor. Uncle Steve was just the same as normal. Ian could not figure it out at all.

'You all right in there?'

'Yes.'

'Well, come on out.'

'Coming.' Ian stumbled out.

'Hungry?'

Ian nodded. It was hours, days since he had eaten.

'What do you fancy?' What Ian fancied was a huge cooked breakfast with ice-cream to follow, but he hardly dared say so.

'Bacon?' he ventured.

'With the trimmings?' Ian nodded. 'You too, Dave? Got room after the toast? Right, I'll nip over to the shop. Get a shower, Ian and we'll have a great nosh-up when I get back.' Uncle Steve left for the shop and Ian showered and got dressed.

'Dave, what's up with him?'

'Nothing.'

'But he's being normal, you know, nice.'

'Yes. He says we've been punished enough already.'

'So what is he going to do?'

'Nothing.'

'Nothing!'

'Well, make us a slap-up meal by the looks of it.'

Uncle Steve returned laden with goodies. He cooked the bacon, sausage, eggs, tomatoes, baked beans and mushrooms and sliced up some crusty white bread. Ian silently sat down to his meal. He did not like to say that he hated mushrooms, so drowned them in brown sauce.

'Ian's waiting for you to do something, Dad. You know, tell us off, punish us.' Ian glowered and tried to kick his cousin but failed, only stubbing his bare toe on the table leg. 'I told him, you said we had been punished enough already.'

'That's right. Must have been awful out there, eh, Ian?'

Ian nodded, unable to speak through his mouthful of egg. It had been awful, terrible. So awful that he did not want to think about it. Uncle Steve seemed to understand.

'Best forget about it, Ian. Do you think, though, you've learned your lesson?'

'Sure thing, Uncle Steve.'

'Well, that'll be an end to that then.'

'What about the police and the warden?'

'Don't worry. You know you were too young to take the boat but it's my boat and I'm not pressing charges. We're all glad you are safe.'

Ian felt as if a great burden had been lifted from him. He had been daft to be so scared and worried. He ought to have known that Uncle Steve would be okay.

'I'll clear up. Here you two, take this money and go and buy yourselves a magazine or two. I'll tidy up. Come back in half an hour.'

Ian and Dave wandered off to the newsagents.

'Dave, why were you crying?'

'Crying. I wasn't!'

'You were, then.'

'Well, not really. It was just, well just, that Dad was nice to me.' Dave felt embarrassed so changed the subject. 'Shall we get Computer Weekly or Boating Monthly?'

'Both.'

They spent the afternoon hanging around the caravan reading. Ian was very achy, especially his arms and legs and he was quite happy to immerse himself in the intricacies of computers or the dimensions of the latest speed boats. Occasionally he glanced at Dave. Fancy crying because you weren't punished. Ian only understood how Dave had felt when Aunt Lynda and the girls returned.

'Yoohoo!' Aunt Lynda burst into the caravan. Bev and Julia followed, looking more exhausted than Ian felt.

'The market was superb . . .'

'And the craft fayre.'

'And we had a lovely picnic up in the hills . . .'

'Wait till you see Aunt Lynda's new jogging suit – purple and lime green.' Ian could wait.

'Got this for you, Ian,' Aunt Lynda passed him a parcel. It was huge. 'Don't panic,' she whispered to Uncle Steve, 'half price in the sale.'

Slowly Ian opened it. Something stiff and blubbery at the same time. Dark and light green. He could not believe it.

'Try it on. I know it's a bit big but you can roll the legs up.'

Ian stripped to his boxer shorts and, still dumb struck, wriggled into the sleeveless wet-suit, slowly closing the strong black zip that ran up the front. He could not believe it. A wet-suit for him! A tear chased another one down his cheek.

'Who's crying now,' whispered Dave, and that did it. Huge sobs shook his body which wobbled away inside the tight green rubber.

'It's lovely. Oh, thank you. Thank you.' Wetly he hugged his aunt, who grinned at him and planted a huge kiss somewhere near his left earhole. Everyone was laughing or crying or talking at once.

'New life jacket for you, Dave. Bev and Julia have got matching trousers and tops. Shirt for you, Steve.' Aunt Lynda was on her knees, diving into bags, throwing stuff everywhere.

It was like Christmas, like a party. Ian was so excited and amazed. He had got it all wrong, when he had lain awake in bed this lunch time. Pinching the boat equalled big trouble. But no. Being rescued and safe equalled lots of fun and happiness. This family would never cease to amaze him.

'Lynda, how much have you spent?'

'Don't fuss, Steve. I'd saved it up. Didn't use the credit card once. I thought it'd make nice early birthday presents.'

Early all right, thought Ian. It was mid-August and his birthday was not until next April. Still he wasn't complaining. A wet-suit of his own! He'd wear it at the swimming baths at home, maybe with some bright orange flippers.

'You're incorrigible,' said Uncle Steve.

'In what?' asked Ian.

'It means incurably bad,' explained his uncle. 'Your aunt is incurable, when it comes to shopping.'

'Good,' Ian grinned. 'I hope that she never gets better.'

'Not much chance of that,' Uncle Steve pretended to sigh, reminding Ian of a deflating balloon.

'Come off it, Steve. You ought to be glad it only happens once or twice a year.'

'Once or twice?'

'Well, not very often anyway. Ignore him, Ian, he

doesn't mean anything,' and Aunt Lynda disappeared to get changed into her new jogging suit.

'Can I go down to the lake?' Ian requested. 'Just for a swim.'

'Thought you'd have gone off lakes for life.'

'I'll be okay, honestly, Uncle Steve.'

'I don't think so, Ian. You and Dave had a lucky escape and I'm amazed you've not got a streaming cold. No water today.'

Ian decided not to protest, but he had got to show his wet-suit off to someone.

'Can I go to the jetty, feed the ducks?'

'Okay. Take care then. Here,' Uncle Steve rummaged in the bin. 'See what they make of the burnt toast.'

Ian set off on the short walk from the caravan to the jetty. It took ages. Heads popped out of caravans.

'You all right, Ian?'

'Don't know how they let you out on your own.'

'How's Dave?'

'Haven't seen that wet-suit before.'

'The worry you gave us . . . If I was your aunt, you wouldn't be able to sit down for a week.'

'Glad you're okay.'

Ian nodded, grinned and grunted at the right places and assured everyone that yes, he was okay, and no, he wouldn't do it again.

He remembered Sunday morning when he had walked down here alone. He had thought then that by the end of the week everyone would know about Ian Rathbone. Well, they did, but not because he was an ace water-skier. But because he was a right fool who had had to be rescued. At least most people were being nice to him, apart from one older woman who would have, 'tanned your hide, if you'd been one of mine.'

There was a lot of activity at the jetty, with boats returning from a day on the lake. Ian continued walking, getting used to the stiff feel of his wet-suit. He followed the curve of the lake, past the open grass where a group of families were pretending they were England's cricket team, and on into the quiet of the woods.

It was cooler here, the shade dappling the sparse grass and dried up undergrowth. Odd bluey gleams shone through the trees, from the lake, and it was fairly quiet. The distant squeals from the water-side receded, along with the repeated 'how's thats' from the cricketers. Sitting down carefully so as not to damage his wet-suit, Ian gazed around him. He was right by the kestrel tree.

I bet she's flying around somewhere, he thought; daft bird, getting trapped like that. Mind you, it wasn't her fault. She wouldn't have known the dangers of flying through trees, a leather cord dangling from her leg. That was the difference, really, between him and the bird. He had known that it was stupid taking the boat, but he had still done it.

Still he and the kestrel had something in common. They had both been trapped. They had both been rescued. Ian was trying to sort his thoughts out, that were tumbling into his brain so fast that they were like tangled spaghetti.

He spoke out loud to himself. 'I got trapped. Then I got rescued, but there was a lot more as well. It was awful out there, I was so scared, I thought they would never find me.' Ian paused and then sat bolt upright. 'Of course, I couldn't rescue myself. Nor could the silly old kestrel. Someone had to find us and get us free; Tom Fraser for the bird, Uncle Steve for me.' He leaned back, chewing a blade of grass. 'But it wasn't just them. It was the Son of Man, God. He got me safe. He found me.' A sort of pulse vibrated through his body. 'He's real! I know he is. God is real. It doesn't matter what my dad thinks, it's true. The Son of Man rescued me.' Ian felt puzzled. 'Is that it? I mean, is that all he does, gets birds out of trees and boys out of lakes? It must mean more than that, but what?' Ian's brain, unaccustomed to such activity, went into overload and gave up. 'I'd better say thanks though.'

Ian shut his eyes but it didn't feel right. Making sure there was no-one around, he got on his knees, facing the tree. Felt more like a prayer that way.

'Hello, God, are you there?' He waited a few seconds, to make sure he had got God's attention. 'It's me, Ian, you know, the boy you found in the lake. Well, I want to say thanks. I really mean it. Thank you ever such a lot. If I knew where you were, I'd write you a letter. I just hope you can hear me.' Ian squatted back on his heels. This kneeling was uncomfortable. 'And if there is more to it, this seeking and saving business, could you let me know what it is? Tara for now.'

Getting up, Ian jogged slowly out of the wood, past the remains of the cricket match and back to the caravan. He could ask Uncle Steve about the seeking and saving, but it didn't seem right somehow. He'd leave it up to God to tell him, if there was anything left to tell.

'Tea-time,' called Bev, sporting her new red and white outfit.

'Salad.'

Ian wolfed his food down quickly. He was surprised how tired he felt. Some of them went to the club, but Ian and Dave sat watching television with Uncle Steve.

'Early night, boys. We're going sight-seeing tomorrow.'

They both groaned.

'In the car! You can't come to the Lake District, Ian, without seeing the hills.'

Can! thought Ian, but said nothing. He would just do what he was told, thankful that he had been let off lightly, after his escapade. If Uncle Steve said hills then that is what they would have. Hundreds of them.

Chapter Nine

Ian had to admit that the Lake District's hills were spectacular. After loading up yet another picnic of vast proportions, they all squashed into the shining grey estate car. Ian was next to the window, in the back and already feeling hot. He wound the window down.

'I told you, you'll boil to death in that thing,' Aunt Lynda commented.

Ian was not going to admit that she was right. The wet-suit was really uncomfortable when it was dry and he was crammed into the car. Still, he was so proud of it he would wear it, if it killed him.

Uncle Steve had worked out a circular route, which involved a lot of stopping, looking and exploring. Through Ambleside and then along the yellow road on the map to Langdale Pikes. For the first time, Ian gazed at the majestic rocky outcrops, clear and barren in the sunlight.

Suddenly they squealed to a stop, reversed and pulled into a car park.

'Dungeon Ghyll Force. You must see it, Ian.'

'We'll all go,' said Aunt Lynda. It was so hot she had taken off the top of her new jogging suit, and in her bright clothes there would be no danger of losing her on the hills.

The rocky path climbed alongside the waterfall which would have been marvellous if there had been more water in it.

'We're nearly dry,' said a rosy-cheeked woman, hanging out her washing at the cottage at the foot of the waterfall. 'I don't know what we'll do if the spring dries up all together.' She glanced at the perfect blue sky. 'Well, at least it's nice for you all.'

Trudging upwards, Ian's breath was coming in rasping gulps. Bev, Julia and Uncle Steve sat down to rest, but the boys and Aunt Lynda continued to climb.

'It's so beautiful here. I love it. You can see for miles.'

Ian turned. It was like a painting. Soft greens and browns merged together and made a contrast to the harsh bare rock and stony slopes. He could see the road winding through the valley and up the pass, and pick out the white stone walls, like rows of teeth, gnashing along the field edges. Ian felt very small surrounded by such grandeur. It was a bit like when he had lain on his back in the lake looking up at the never-ending sky.

They returned to the car.

'Next stop Blea Tarn. Ian, aren't you hot?'

'Yes, Aunt Lynda.' Sweat was dripping off him.

'Well your shorts and T-shirt are on top of the picnic. Here, put them on.'

With Dave's help Ian forced himself out of the wet-suit. It was like unrolling an Egyptian mummy. His body was bright red with sweaty heat.

'You pong,' commented Dave.

'Too bad!' Ian was relieved to be in normal clothes. Thank goodness he had not got to wear the wet-suit all day.

Blea Tarn was near a car park at the top of the pass. It was ace. A perfect blue round lake with dark green spires of fir trees merging with glossy rhododendron bushes on the far side. Fortunately there was a flat path, and Ian and Dave decided to walk right round the lake. They could tell it was normally muddy as deep sheep footprints were solidified into the pale dried out mud. It was like being on top of the world.

After lunch they paddled at the edge but it was freezing cold. The cousins made a circle of stepping stones and then had a competition to see who could go round them the quickest. There was much pushing and shoving to make each other fall off and be disqualified, and a lot of laughs. Uncle Steve decided to join in.

'What's the record?'

'Thirteen point seven seconds.'

'I'll beat that easy.'

'But you've got trainers on. That's not fair. We've got bare feet.'

'Well I'm not taking them off! Right, Dave, start timing me . . . now.'

Uncle Steve set off on the wobbly wet stones as if he was in the hundred metre sprint at the Olympics. Leap . . . wobble . . . big step . . . bigger wobble . . . and over he went, bottom first into six inches of cold lake.

Everyone was helpless with laughter. Dave kept on counting . . . 'Twenty-seven, twenty-eight, come on, Dad, you'll never beat the record like this.'

Trying to get up, Uncle Steve slipped again and sprawled like a stranded fish, on his stomach in the water. The others heaved him out, water streaming from his best light-blue jeans and oozing out of his white leather trainers.

Aunt Lynda told him off, which made them laugh even more. Then she made him change into his own swimming trunks and her purple and green top.

He insisted on driving barefoot. 'Can't trust you, Lynda, with these lanes,' and he tied his jeans onto the roof rack so that they would blow in the air and dry out. They wound their way down the mountain pass, the jeans like a demented banner on the roof, and along to

Coniston Water. Here they forced Uncle Steve to stay hidden in the car, while they refuelled on ice-creams and wandered around the village, in and out of the little shops and streets.

Ian sat on a bench, next to the grey stone plaque which commemorated Donald Campbell's attempt at the world water-speed record. He had died in the attempt years ago, but Ian felt a strange shiver as he thought of the brave man who had met his end in a watery grave. I nearly met the same fate on Tuesday night, thought Ian. Only I was stupid not brave. As he finished his rum and raisin ice-cream with double chocolate flake, he wondered what made Donald Campbell do it. What made anyone do anything? After all what made Uncle Steve love the Lake District so much, or Aunt Lynda like shopping? He sighed. Or his own mum and dad want to fight and yell? Why couldn't they be happy and have fun like his aunt and uncle? Ian was having trouble deleting the thoughts from his brain, so he got up and rejoined the others.

'We'll drive back slowly, and then we thought we'd go up the Kirkstone Pass and have some tea at the ancient inn there,' Aunt Lynda informed them.

Ian didn't mind, but one hill was starting to look very much like another by now. He had rather hoped that Uncle Steve would return to the caravan after his duck-ing. Then there would have been a chance to go out on the boat. But no such luck. Hills and more hills.

Eventually they climbed to the top of the Kirkstone Pass and pulled up at the inn's gravel car park, perched on a bit of flat land.

'Bit early for tea,' Aunt Lynda said. 'I'm all for sun-bathing. What about the rest of you?'

'Me too,' chorused Bev and Julia.

'I'll read my book.' Ian was relieved that Uncle Steve had put his damp jeans back on.

'Me and Ian'll go exploring. Come on. Ian.'

In front of them curved another huge hill. It looked just like the ones that little children draw, with rounded sides. The grass was so short and frizzled up by the sun and the sheep grazing, that it reminded Ian of a haircut.

'Let's climb to the top of old skin-head,' said Dave.

The top got further away with every minute. The boys kept on going, refusing either to look down to see how far they had come, or up to see how far they had to go. Both were breathing noisily, and were wet with sweat, but neither would give up until the other one did. Reaching a little hollow they both collapsed at the same time, giggling and trying to get their breath back to normal.

Dave, of course, had been here before and was busy pointing out all the hills and tiny blue dots that were lakes. Ian noticed that Coniston Old Man appeared to have three different locations and that Ambleside seemed to have shifted somewhat. He was not really listening until Dave caught his attention.

'And that's Windermere.'

'What?'

'That bit down there. Look, follow my arm. See?'

Ian laid his head along Dave's arm and squinted at the patch of light blue.

'You sure? I mean it's so tiny.'

'Well, it's only a bit of it.'

'But you can't see the boats, not even the lake steamers, from up here.'

'True . . . and that's where we set up camp the other day.'

But Ian was off in a world of his own. The vast lake looked so minute. He could not see any details. A sense of amazement spread over him. He, Ian, couldn't see anything, but Tuesday night, God had seen him, just one boy, in the middle of the lake. And it had been dark. God must have x-ray vision.

'Dave,' he interrupted his cousin's monologue. 'When we were stuck on the lake, did you pray, you know, talk to God?'

'Course. Did you?'

'Well, er,' Ian avoided answering. 'Anyway, how did God know where we were?'

'He knows everything.'

'Everything?'

'Yes. He even knows what we think and what we are going to do.'

Ian fell silent. Perhaps he could ask Dave about the seeking and saving bit, but he didn't know how to put it into words.

'Dave,' he began, 'God, this Son of Man, the seeking and saving bit. Well he did that for us, didn't he? I mean we got saved, rescued.'

'Yes,' Dave wasn't sure where this conversation was heading. All he knew was that he wanted Ian to believe what he did, but he did not want to push his own beliefs onto his cousin.

'Is that all there is to it?'

'All there is to what?'

'The Son of Man coming to seek and save the lost. I mean does he just find boys and rescue kestrels, or what?'

Dave turned to Ian. 'Well, it's more than that. Do you want me to explain?'

'Have a go.'

'Well we are all lost, or trapped, like the bird . . .'

'How?' Ian interrupted.

'The Bible calls it sin. It's all the wrong things we think and do, but mostly it's because we ignore God and just do our own thing. It makes us lost.'

'Then what?'

'Well, we have to be found, rescued. That's where Jesus, you know, the Son of Man, comes in. He came to earth, died on a cross, came alive again, and if we trust him, he rescues us.'

'Like Tom Fraser did with the kestrel?'

'Yes, you've got the idea,' Dave was warming up now.
'You see, when the bird was rescued, Tom could set her
free. And that's what Jesus does. He gets us free of the
bad things we have done.'

'But you took the boat as well, Dave. You're a Christian and you did something wrong.'

'I know. Being a Christian doesn't magically make you
do everything right. You still muck it up. But Jesus is
there, on your side, and if you say sorry, he carries on
being your friend.'

Ian thought. He liked the idea of being a friend of
Jesus, of having a friend who knew everything, could
rescue you and be there to talk to. But how could he be
Jesus' friend? Ian knew that he had never even thought
about God for twelve years, until he was stuck in the
lake. Would God want to be his friend?'

'Does he want to be anyone's friend?'

'Course. More than anything.'

'Mine?'

'Yes, if you ask him, that's all, you know, Ian. You
just talk to him and ask him.'

Far below the purply-green splodge that was Aunt
Lynda was waving.

'Food-time,' Dave jumped up. 'Race you down!'

Ian was thoughtful. 'I'll be down in a bit. Order pie
and chips for me.'

He watched his cousin bobbing down the hill. Some
of what Dave had said made sense. Ian knew he wanted
Jesus to be his friend, to find him properly. Dave had
said that all he had to do was to ask him.

So for the third time in two days Ian decided to talk
to God.

'It's me again – Ian. Hello.' He paused. 'I don't get
all of this stuff but I do want to be your friend. I'm

sorry I've ignored you for twelve years and,' he counted on his fingers, 'nearly four months. I don't want to ignore you any more so will you be my friend? Thanks.'

Ian got up and walked slowly down the hill, splaying out his toes inside his trainers to keep his balance. He was not sure how he felt. It seemed to be mainly relief, but also pleasure that some things were starting to make sense.

His pie and chips were waiting for him in the inn's old interior. It was dark after the glare outside and it took Ian's eyes some time to accustom themselves to the worn stone floors, old dark tables, low beamed ceiling and clutter of plates and ornaments on every available surface.

He ate his food quietly and ordered apple pie and cream for afters.

'You all right, Ian?' asked Aunt Lynda, reaching across her Black Forest gateau to feel his forehead. 'Not got a touch of the sun, I hope.'

'I'm fine. Bit tired. You know, the hill.'

'Do you know,' said Dave, who was back in his tourist guide mood, 'that this is called the Kirkstone Pass because there's a rock that looks like a church. And kirk is another word for church. Didn't see it myself, though.'

Nor me, thought Ian. But that hillside was like a church. It was special. It was where he had talked to God. And now he felt he could talk to him lots, any time, anywhere.

As Aunt Lynda dawdled over her second coffee, Dave and Ian wandered outside. The hillsides were shot with purples and shadowy pinks and the sun slowly lowered itself, like an old lady in a comfortable chair, behind the far mountains.

'I asked him,' Ian said quietly.

Dave smiled. 'That's great.' Ian was pleased that Dave

had understood. He didn't really want to talk about it any more but he wanted Dave to know what had happened.

'Last day for me and Julia tomorrow.'

'You've got most of Saturday as well.'

'Yes, but Friday's really the last day. Do you think your dad will take us out on the boat?'

'Sure, he's already told me so. And he's got a surprise.'

'A surprise. Who for?'

'You.'

'Tell me.' But however much he badgered Dave, Ian could not find out what lay in store for him tomorrow.

Chapter Ten

Friday started much the same as any of the other days of the holiday – everyone banging into each other as they got up and helped themselves to breakfast. Croissants today. Ian enjoyed the taste of the warm flaky pastry and melted butter as he ate three of them, washed down by a tall glass of orange juice. Bits dropped everywhere but he flicked them off his bare chest onto the floor, until Aunt Lynda banished him outside.

'Dave, you and Ian can go and uncover the boat. Uncover! Nothing else, understand?'

'Right, Dad. Are we taking a picnic?'

'Not today.' Ian's heart sank. No picnic meant that they could not be going out for long. This family only went a few hours between gigantic meals, not that Ian usually minded. But if they were only out until lunch-time, he might not get a go in the water.

'And put your wet-suits on! I know its boiling already, ut you'll need them.' Uncle Steve shouted out of the caravan door. Ian's hopes lifted as he forced himself into the green pipe-like legs of his own wet-suit.

By now experts at boat uncovering, the boys sat on the seats, waiting for the rest of the family to invade. The boat moved gently on the moorings. Eventually Uncle Steve appeared, started the engine and called, 'Cast off. Ian, watch that side. Dave, mind the front.'

Ian wondered where the others were, but did not ask

in case his uncle decided to wait for them. To his horror they turned south, away from the skiing area, cruising at a snail's pace. They refuelled at the marina in Bowness and just stayed there doing nothing.

'What are we doing?' Ian asked, as Dave did not seem bothered, but his uncle did not reply.

'I thought you said ten o'clock?' Dave queried.

'Well, it's only just gone ten now. He'll be here in a minute.' He started to wave to a tall thin grey man, who was hurrying towards them.

'Hi, Tom, what kept you?'

'Couldn't find my suit.' Tom Fraser, alias Batman, patted the grey rubber that covered him from head to toe. 'Hello, lads, gorgeous day, isn't it?' and he climbed into the boat.

'Up the top, near the western shore okay?' asked Uncle Steve.

'Best place. Very calm. Ideal.'

'Ideal for what?' Ian interrupted, only to be answered by another, 'You'll see!'

They reached the water-skiing area and Tom got ready to ski as Uncle Steve unpacked the tow-rope.

'You two, act as observers. Okay, Tom?' and the grey eel-shape flipped into the water.

Ian was annoyed. 'You said it would be a surprise for me,' he hissed to Dave as they let the rope out through their fingers. 'Him coming is a surprise, but I thought it was supposed to be something nice for me!'

Dave just grinned, giving a smug look, to show he knew something which Ian didn't. Ian was desperate with curiosity, but nothing exciting was happening, at least not to him.

Tom was up on his skis, floating over the water, one-handed, swooping and swirling, like the gulls did when they fed them picnic remains from the boat. He was ace. His fantastic skill did nothing to make Ian feel better.

It just rubbed it in that he could not ski at all, let alone like a bird. The boat slowed down quite near the shore. Turning back to fetch Tom, Uncle Steve passed Ian a buoyancy jacket.

'Your turn.' At last the magic words. 'Come on, what are you waiting for?'

'Tom's still in the water.'

'I know. Get in and join him.'

Once again the cold water made him quickly shiver but Ian was not bothered. His own wet-suit was wet for the first time.

'Now what?' he called, bobbing around. He noticed that he could see the bottom.

'Do what Tom tells you,' and Uncle Steve carefully took the boat into deeper water, leaving Ian in the hands of the mad water-skiing, kestrel-rescuing vicar, who was grinning short-sightedly at him.

'Right. We'll get the skis on. Stand up.' Ian was surprised to touch the bottom. And with much pulling and grunting the wayward polished planks of wood were fastened to his feet.

'Now, you know the correct position?'

'Yes, but I can never get it.'

'You will. Try now, while I'm holding you . . . That's it . . . bend your knees a bit more . . . I'll keep the skis steady . . . arms straight. Look up, where you are going, not in the water.'

'I always go in the water!'

'Not today, you don't! Now, when I say, give your uncle a signal and have a go.'

'I can't do it.' Funny, Ian did not mind admitting his fears to Tom.

'You can. I'll be holding you. Help you balance.'

'But he can't tow two of us.'

'I'll let go at the right moment. I've been doing this since before you were born. Trust me?'

Ian looked into the wet face near his. He may as well trust Tom. He did not have any other options.

'Ready? Call your uncle.'

'Go! Hit it!' yelled Ian at the top of his voice.

Once again he felt the familiar pull on his arms and the force on his legs but this time he did not wobble or fall over. He got up, supported by Tom, and then fell over, landing with his customary acrobatic splash. Tom swam across to him.

'Better?'

'Yes, I nearly did it. Can I try again?'

'You can try all morning. I've got until twelve-thirty.'

All morning! Ian realised that this must be the surprise. Uncle Steve had found someone who could help him. A surge of confidence poured over him. He'd do it!

And he did! After many attempts, each time patiently assured by Tom, and balanced by him at the critical take-off point, Ian was up. And he stayed up, leaning his body slightly backwards, arms straight, knees bent. At last he could feel the exhilaration of gliding, well – of bumping over the water, the spray tickling his face and bare arms. He did not need to imagine what it was like. He knew. Ian was not aware of the fact that he laughed out loud, even as his run came to a sudden halt and he tumbled into the foaming lake.

'I did it! I did it!'

'Great,' Dave called. 'Climb aboard. We'll take you back to Tom. It's too far to swim.' Ian glanced towards the shore. He had skied right across the curve of the bay. All that way, by himself. He felt fantastic.

Twice more he repeated his feat, getting increasingly excited.

'On your own, now,' said Tom, slithering into the boat. 'Don't think about it, just do it. It's like riding a bike. Once you've learned, you don't forget.'

So Ian waited to ski all on his own. Tom was right. He was up and flying some way before crash landing as usual.

'Time to go,' Uncle Steve called, as the boat returned for him. Happily Ian clambered aboard, aware of how tired, and more importantly, how hungry, he was. As the boat streaked back to the marina, Ian felt like hugging himself, he was so happy. His dream had come true. Ian Rathbone could water-ski! Wait till he told Julia and the others.

Over lunch, huge sandwiches crammed with cheese and pickle, Ian told and retold his story, splash by splash. He was so excited he even forgot to eat.

'I knew you'd do it!' said Aunt Lynda. 'So I got us this.' She produced a cake with pink 'Congratulations' on it and pink iced flowers around the edge. 'I know it's a bit, well, pink, but it was all I could find in Bowness this morning.'

'It's great!' said Ian. He cut it up, while Julia took some more photos. He didn't mind if the cake looked like one for a baby, and a girl at that, it was the message that counted. Congratulations! Well done! I'm a super hero, he thought!

'It was good of Tom to help out,' said Aunt Lynda. 'Shame he had a meeting and couldn't join us for lunch.'

As she was talking, Ian realised that in his excitement and the rush to get Tom back on time, he had not thanked him.

'I didn't really say thank you,' he said.

'Well, why don't you write him a note, pop it through his door. Take a piece of cake as well.'

'It'll get squashed.'

'I'll wrap it up.'

Ian carefully composed his thank you note, drawing a passable likeness of a boat and skier. 'And I thought you'd like to know that I've been rescued and made friends with the Son of Man, Jesus,' he added. After all, if he had not been made to go to church, he would never have heard Tom talk about the seeking and saving, and maybe he would have never believed that God was there, waiting to be his friend.

'What are we doing this afternoon?' he asked.

'Whatever you like. About fiveish we'll have a snack and go out on the boat for a ride. Then we'll have another pizza tonight.' Uncle Steve yawned. 'Now, I'm putting my feet up for a bit. Boys, wash up and disappear.'

Ian decided to take his letter to Tom's and Dave trailed after him. They were just trying to stuff the cake through the letter-box, when the door opened. Tom was smart in clean trousers and short-sleeved shirt and Ian blinked to make sure that this was the same man that had wetly helped him all morning.

'Ah, Ian and Dave. Just in time. Kettle's about to boil,' and Tom led the way into the kitchen which was even more untidy than on their last visit.

'I've come to say thank you,' began Ian, 'and I'm not thirsty,' he added, as the tin of evaporated milk appeared to be added to the mugs of black tea. Too late. Ian sipped the revolting brew. How Tom's insides stood up to the daily onslaught of this concoction was beyond him.

'It was a pleasure.' Tom looked up from reading the note. 'You looked so happy when you got up on the skis.'

'I was. Thanks ever so.'

'What's this bit about being a friend of Jesus?' Tom asked casually.

'Well, after the kestrel, and the rescue and up in the mountains, and Dave telling me about not ignoring God, and climbing Old Skinhead and seeing Windermere so little below, and all that. Well then I did it.'

'Did it?' Tom was not sure what Ian was talking about.

'You know, asked him to be my friend. The Son of Man. The rescuer.'

'Great,' Tom was thoughtful. 'And he'll be your friend always, Ian. When you go home, when you go back to school,' Ian groaned, 'whatever happens.' He jumped up. 'Got to go. Visiting the sick. Want to come?'

Not likely, thought Ian. Sick people on holiday!

'It's old Mrs Reed, up at Manor Top Farm. It's her son who keeps the kestrels.' Ian looked at Dave. 'I expect you could see them.'

'Great!'

'Well, run and ask your mum, Dave. We won't be gone long.'

Ten minutes later they were bouncing along a rutted path in Tom's old Landrover to the farm. Jumping out, Tom yelled, 'Stewart, Stewart Reed! Anyone at home?'

A gangling man of about forty appeared wearing enormous wellington boots, although all the mud had long dried up in the scorching sun.

'Tom! Good to see you. Mother will be pleased. And who are these two ruffians?'

'Dave and Ian. They are the ones who found your bird.'

'Good work there, lads. Do you want to see her?'

'Yes, please.'

'I'll go and see your mother,' said Tom, moving towards the old stone farmhouse. 'Make us a cuppa as well.' Ian groaned quietly. He would never drink tea again in his life.

Mr Reed led them through the barn, past a steaming heap of manure topped by a cloud of flies, and into another old building that was surprisingly light and airy. Huge cages lined one wall and the boys could see the birds, each one glaring at them, following their every move.

'I'll get Jessie out.'

'Jessie?'

'The one you rescued. My own fault. I'd taken her to a field lower down to fly. She wasn't used to it and I thought she was lost for good.' Mr Reed donned a pair of thick leather gloves, fastened a cord to the ring on Jessie's leg, and brought the bird outside into the field.

'Want to see her go?'

They nodded and Jessie flew effortlessly in circles above their heads, her wings outstretched, gliding on tiny air currents that they could not even feel. Mr Reed whistled and the bird plummeted out of the sky and landed on his wrist.

'Want to hold her?'

'You bet.' Dave and Ian fetched more gloves and both were fascinated by being so close to the beautiful bird that they had found. If they had not rescued her, this free flying machine would have been dead, rotating from a tree branch. Ian was glad that Jessie was safe.

'Tea-time!' Tom's voice was clear. Must come from shouting all those sermons in church. Ian managed to sip some of his drink before they left to return to Bowness. He was really pleased that they had seen Jessie alive and well.

Kestrels and hills, Windermere and water-skiing, food, lots of it, his own wet-suit. What a holiday this was! Ian felt sad. What a holiday this had been! It was nearly over now. He hadn't even got photos of the best bits, the skiing this morning and the bird flying just now. But Ian did not think he would need photographs to remind him of his week at Windermere. He didn't even need his diary, which he had forgotten to write since the first day. He would never forget all that had happened.

Ian went to a couple of shops and bought his mum some Lakeland fudge and his dad a model of a speed boat. From the postcard rack he selected a picture of the Kirkstone Pass, his special place, to keep somewhere safe. Then he went back to the caravan determined to enjoy the rest of the day.

As he got ready for bed, Uncle Steve came up to him. 'This is for you, Ian. Dave told me what happened on the hillside. It'll help if you read a bit of this every day and talk to Jesus. I've written down some suggestions for where to start.'

Ian took the Bible gratefully and slid his Kirkstone Pass postcard into it. He had seen his uncle's family quietly reading their Bibles in the mornings. He could do the same. Then he could get to know his new friend better.

As he fell asleep a thought struck Ian. What would Dad say if he saw the Bible? Another thought quickly followed. And what would Mum and Dad be like when they came for him and Julia tomorrow?

Chapter Eleven

Ian woke very early and tiptoed out of the caravan just taking time to grab a sweater and pair of jeans. Quietly he pulled them on over his pyjamas and found his trainers.

His last day! Ian felt sad and pleased at the same time. Sad that the wonderful week was nearly over, pleased that soon he would see his mum and dad, but also a bit scared. What if they were no different? That would be awful. Anyway, he would not think about them now.

Ian set off to say goodbye to all his favourite places. He might never see them again and he wanted to remember exactly what they were like. That way he could keep the pictures of them forever in his mind. It was important that he visited them on his own, so he could concentrate without the hustle and bustle of the rest of the family.

He sat down at the jetty. Even the ducks were not awake yet, but the swan glared at him suspiciously.

'You're lucky,' said Ian. 'living here all year, getting fat and paddling up and down.' He reached out his hand to stroke the damp snake-like neck. It was a mistake and the old swan hissed and spat at him. Ian hissed back but the swan stood his ground and it was Ian who decided to retreat. He wouldn't miss the old bird.

Ian wandered off through the wood again, stopping by the kestrel tree. With much grunting, and a rip in the knee of his jeans, he climbed part way up. Wedged with his back against the trunk and his feet on the same branch Jessie had been caught on, Ian pretended he was a kestrel. Flapping his arms, he breathed as fast as he could and turned his head about to search for prey. He tried a soft whistle at the same time.

'Weee – I can see you. I'm swooping now. Got you!'

'You all right up there?' An elderly man, walking his dog, looked anxiously up the tree. 'Not stuck are you?'

'I'm fine. Playing.' Ian felt a right fool. He could hardly explain that he was a kestrel. He fixed his eyes on the man's retreating back before carefully getting out of the tree. Patting its rough bark, he said goodbye and carried on until he came to a quiet spot where he could look over the lake.

'Bye, Windermere. I'll be back. When I'm older. I'll buy a boat and live here and have loads of money and go skiing all the time.' He squatted on his heels, trailing his hands in the tongues of silky water gently licking the edge, unaware that his trainers were getting wet. He wished he had a bottle with him. Then he could take a drop of Lake Windermere back home. Instead he chose a smooth black pebble and put it in his pocket. He would keep it forever.

Tracing his way back to the caravan, Ian stopped and chatted to other holidaymakers who were out and about.

'I can ski now!' He must have said it ten times and each time it became more real to him. It might be years before he got the chance to ski again, but no-one could ever take away the fact that he had done it. He was still smiling to himself when he reached the caravan.

'I'll make breakfast.' He filled six bowls with cereal, using up all the last bits in the boxes, and topped them with milk, natural yoghurt and chopped nuts. Sliced banana and a handful of dried fruit completed his masterpieces, which were greeted with some strange looks by the others. Everyone ate them, though.

'What's happening?'

'You and Julia can take your dirty stuff to the laundrette, and then pack your clothes. Save your mum a job.' Aunt Lynda informed him. Ian groaned inwardly but quietly bribed Julia to do it with a pound coin. Julia was broke, having spent most of her money on earrings and make-up, while Ian had used very little of his cash. He was going to start saving for a speed-boat. Mind you they were thousands of pounds, and it might take a while.

'Your mum and dad will be here about one, so we'll have a barbeque.' Aunt Lynda went off to buy food and Ian was left washing salad and drying it by shaking it all over Dave. Then he put the barbeque together and Uncle Steve took hours getting it alight. At last there were no other jobs to do and Ian was sent to wait at the caravan park entrance for his parents.

He counted the cars, said hello to everyone, until the dusty blue Escort came noisily down the road. Dad still had not got the exhaust fixed. It had been on its last legs for months. He hopped into the back, staring at his parents' heads, to see if they were any different. It was hard to tell.

'You had a nice time, Ian?' His mum turned. She was tanned golden brown and even had freckles on her nose. Her hair was curlier than usual and blonder. She must have had it done.

'Great!'

'Didn't get into trouble, eh?' That was Dad doing a racing car halt by the caravan, sending clouds of dust into the barbeque which spluttered but carried on bravely flickering. Ian was glad that he did not have to reply, as there was a tide of greetings, back-slappings and hugs.

'You're looking great, Carol.' Aunt Lynda hugged Ian's mum. 'You and Jeff have a good time?'

'So so, I'll tell you later.' Ian's mum looked at him

and Aunt Lynda got the message. Ian was not going to find out what 'so so' meant. 'Where's Julia?'

'Here, Mum.' Julia appeared in her new outfit.

'My, you look grown up.'

'I *am* grown up!'

Ian's dad was telling Uncle Steve all about the hold up on the motorway and how much petrol the car was using. Just like normal. Just the same. Ian watched as his dad flicked beefburgers onto the barbeque. He loved the smell as the fat dripped onto the hot charcoal under the grill. They all sat around eating until no-one could manage another bite.

'Well then,' said Ian's dad, patting his stomach with appreciation. 'I'll say this for you, Lynda, you always know how to feed a crowd. How's the terror been?'

This was it. Ian waited. What would Dad say when he knew that Ian had pinched the boat?

'Fine. We had a great week. One or two adventures, eh, Ian?'

'Yes, Uncle Steve.' Ian waited for his uncle to catalogue the things he did wrong but nothing happened. 'Show your dad your wet-suit.'

Ian got it out and proudly strutted up and down in it.

'You can ski then?'

'Yes, Dad, it's brill.'

'Easy?'

'Well . . . I could do it in the end. Tom Fraser helped me.'

'Tom who?'

'He's the vicar.'

'Vicar. A water-skiing vicar!' Dad looked at him sternly. 'You've not been hanging around vicars all week, have you?'

'It's not like that, Dad.'

'Well, what is it like?'

'He's nice, and he made me think about being rescued.

With the kestrel and Skinhead mountain and Jesus being my friend.' Ian felt scared. What would Dad say?

'What on earth are you talking about?' Dad had not got a clue what Ian's garbled sentences meant and Ian was relieved when he quickly changed the subject by asking his uncle if they could have a trip on the boat.

The eight of them squeezed into the boat and slowly pottered along the shore.

'This is our beach.'

'Mum, I biscuited here. It was ace.'

'You ought to see Uncle Steve on the skis.'

'And Dave!'

'And me!' added Ian.

'No time for that today.'

Ian was glad really. He did not want to try to ski in front of all this lot. He might mess it up. He wanted to remember yesterday, his high spot, when he'd done it and done well.

'About here we rescued them.'

'Rescued? Who?' and so the whole story came out. Ian was amazed. His dad seemed to think it was funny but then he had not been out here in the dark choppy water scared to death.

'Well, fancy you having it in you,' he slapped Ian on the back. 'Guts you've got, my son, guts.' Dad obviously had not heard all the details of the story and Ian was certainly not going to fill them in for him! Let him think it was exciting, not stupid.

They moored and picked up the bags at the caravan. Uncle Steve was staying until tomorrow, so he and his family waved the others off. Ian was trying not to cry and managed to succeed. The wonder and magic of the holiday was fading as he sat in the back of the rumbling car heading southwards.

'I told you, head for a junction further down.'

'You know nothing, woman. Who's driving?'

'But you wanted to avoid the hold up.'

'It'll have been cleared hours ago.'

'If you follow this road here,' Ian's mum thrust a flapping map under his dad's nose, 'you can join the motorway here.'

'Carol, if we relied on your map-reading abilities, we'd get nowhere.' Dad called over his shoulder. 'You know we've been touring North Wales. Well, your mum here made sure we saw a lot more of it than we intended. Up and down the same roads, through the same villages, always looking out of the window instead of at the map.'

'But, Jeff, it was so pretty, the hills, and little cottages. And everywhere began with Ll . . . I couldn't tell one from another.'

They droned on as Ian sat sadly watching the hills and lakes go further into the distance until they were only smudges on the horizon behind him. It was almost as if they were no longer real, just something he had imagined. This was reality. Mum and Dad arguing as usual. Mind you, Dad wasn't shouting quite as loud as normal and Mum was even giggling a bit.

Ian knew they would not tell him what was going on. He only knew his parents were unhappy because of the rows, slamming doors and by listening outside the living room door when they thought he was in bed. He could hardly say, 'By the way, are you two splitting up?' when he wasn't even supposed to know that there was a problem.

Julia was asleep when they stopped at the motorway service station for a late tea, but she woke up and revived over yet another pie and chips. Dad treated them all to huge ice-creams.

'It's good to have you both back,' he said, a bit gruffly. 'Missed you, didn't we, Carol?'

'Like toothache!' Mum grinned. 'No seriously, it's nice to be back to normal with everything the same.'

Nice for them, thought Ian. I don't know what normal is any more. Everything isn't the same. It might be for them, but I hope not. I hope they stop fighting. I hope we'll have some fun together, but I don't know if they'll change.

And that, Ian realised was the difference. Everything wasn't the same because he had changed. It wasn't just that he could water-ski, had a superb tan, felt really fit and had even whiter blond hair. It was something to do with becoming a friend of Jesus. Ian felt a flicker of happiness. There was one thing he had not left behind at Windermere. Well, one person – Jesus. Ian could talk to him anywhere: at home, in the café, in the car. And he could tell him about anything. After all, what had Dave said? God knew everything. Well then, he could talk to him about Mum and Dad and the rows, and about missing the Lake District, and about school, and wanting to ski again and . . . and . . . and . . . The list could go on forever.